Sporty Spec

Sporty Spec
Games of the Fantastic

Edited by
Karen A. Romanko

Raven Electrick Ink

First edition, October 2007

ISBN 978-0-6151-7361-0

Raven Electrick Ink
http://ravenelectrick.com
comments@ravenelectrick.com

For Dad and my late Mom, for Butch and Jayne,
my home team

For Bob,
and a first date of racquetball that led to a lasting match

Contents

Introduction

Sports and games are with us from the moment we first learn to keep score. From hopscotch to Little League, from video game tournaments to golf dates, from Sunday-morning quarterbacking to Monday-night bingo, the lure of championship, the quest for skill and perfection, the electricity of cheering for a common cause, all hold appeals most of us can't resist.

Sometimes, to be sure, sports and games are merely pleasant diversions. But in other, rare and transcendent moments, sports and games form the indelible memories and markers of our lives—a first game of catch with Dad, learning chess from an older sister, watching a miracle on ice or a curse reversed.

In *Sporty Spec: Games of the Fantastic*, sports and games are still with us, in prophesied futures, parallel presents, and imagined pasts. From a tennis match with Death to a chess game with Oberon, from free throws with the Fairy Court to surfing with werewolves, every sport imaginable (and a few unimaginable) exist within our speculative city of games.

Forty-two authors, veterans and rookies alike, have contributed flash fiction and poetry that will take you from pong with a dust mote at the beginning of the world to sailboarding through the stars at the universe's edge. Along the way, the contributors examine the nature of competition, the impact of cheating, the effects of technology, the aftermath of injury, the role of gender, and "real world" themes, such as climatic change, political repression, and terrorism.

But we haven't forgotten the laughter and joy of play, and some of the pieces are just goofy fun, like a game of slapjack.

From baseball in hell to ice-skating in the heavens, there are no sports like these, and I invite you to be a spectator at our speculative games.

Karen A. Romanko
Los Angeles, California
October 2007

The Sport of Kings

Paul Abbamondi

Wesley took a chance, betting on Autumn Spirit, and all his friends hooted and howled. The warstallions and hyperpulse c-steeds zipped forward at the sound of the gunshot, leaving the slow-trotting horse and rider half a mile back in a dusty haze.

"Come on!" Wesley stood from his seat and shook a fist at the track.

"You could've just given me the hundred chips, you know," one of his friends said, slapping him on the shoulder. "Or, you know, bet on something *built* for speed."

He shook his friend's hand away. "I don't care about enhancements and cyber-widgets—"

"Or money, for that matter!"

"Whatever."

Turning his attention back to the race, squinting hard through the floating ads and the hovering cheerleaders, he locked onto his horse. The rider, according to the data streamed earlier, was a young girl from the suburbs, just like Wesley. When he saw that her horse had been born pure and untainted in an actual hay-laden barn, something told him he'd found a winner. Everyone ignored the underdog, everyone but one adventurer, and to him go the spoils.

A commentator rumbled, his voice reverberating throughout the stadium: "Look!"

Wesley turned his eyes off Autumn Spirit momentarily, only to look farther up the track, where the cluster of silver-armored horses sped along with ease. A shadow exploded behind it, black tendrils slipping out like writhing snakes, and then a great mare burst down and through its competition. A trail of smoke followed.

"Why! That's KingTech Lorroin's steed! Nightshade! He calls her Nightshade!"

"Nightshade," Wesley murmured, returning his focus to the only real rider-animal combo out there. She was picking up pace; or the cluster ahead was slowing down. They seemed to be on the fritz. The smoky horse ahead of them glided along the track like a cloud, hovering low and moving with purpose. It would soon lap Autumn Spirit.

"Move! Move!" he shouted. "Ride, ride!"

"Oh give it up," his friend said with a sneer, "least you have a legit excuse. Your horse is boring; that demon steed, that's not fair. Not even on the race roster!"

Wesley ignored him. Nightshade passed Autumn Spirit, moving confidently forward and passing again through the cluster of enhanced horses. They slowed down more, so much that Autumn Spirit was now even with them.

Everyone around him in the stands cursed and threw trash. No, not trash. Tickets, they were ripping up their tickets. Wesley held on to his tight.

The horses were on the third and final lap now: Nightshade in the lead, Autumn Spirit halfway back, and everyone else moving like turtles in mud. Wesley leaned against the railing, fixed on the race. If he was sweating, he didn't have time to realize it.

Calculating the distance between the horses and the finish line, Wesley felt heavy and disheartened. Nightshade was too far ahead, making a victory near-impossible. Least his girls beat a bunch of automatons.

On its last sweep of the track, the KingTech's horse from the void passed through the slowing cluster before exploding into a crackling puff of smoke and lightning. As the air cleared and the roar of the crowd reached a deafening level, all became obvious.

The demon steed was gone, the six or seven enhanced horses back frozen in the track, their joints stiff and void of life, and Autumn Spirit rushing forward at a solid pace. Her rider pulled a saffron-colored flag from her shirt and waved it wildly as they jetted across the finish line.

As the crowd booed relentlessly, Wesley slipped away to claim his winnings.

"Wait up!"

Wesley stuffed the bulging envelop of chips under his shirt and turned, expecting to see the soured faces of his roommates. Instead, an old man using a cane hobbled over, his bushy brows lifting with excitement.

"Yeah?"

Taking his cane, the old man poked at Wesley's stomach. "You bet on her, on the autumn mare. How'd you know?"

"Know what?"

"That she was *solid*."

He shrugged. "I like the underdogs."

"Me too." They walked out of the stadium together. In the parking lot were men and women, huddled in angry arrays and broke from the race. Wesley hurried over to his car, the old man still shuffling by behind him.

"You come to the races every week?" Wesley asked.

"Just about," he said with a wave, turning to depart. Only now did Wesley see that he only had a cane in hand. No clinking envelope of chips. Zero winnings.

"Hold on. I thought you wagered on Autumn Spirit, too?"

The old man smiled, showing three teeth, one of which glittered. "Me? I'm not allowed to bet. Contract says so." He bowed slightly and snapped his fingers. To his right, a shadow exploded, scattering everyone in the area. Except for Wesley. He clung to his ride and watched as the mare Nightshade burst out, circled round, and scooped the old man up and onto her back in a single fluid motion.

"You're...you're the KingTech!" Wesley barely made the words out. Up close, Nightshade was a living, pulsing being—black as black gets, and already he could feel her sapping his strength.

"Lorroin, and while you may like the underdogs, lucky boy, don't go betting on them for some time now. Eh?"

Before Wesley could reply, Nightshade leapt into the sky and disappeared, leaving only a swirling trail of smoke behind. He took out the envelope and stared at it, knowing Autumn Spirit truly hadn't won, would never win, not without someone's help or through someone else's failures. It made the money empty. He took out what he'd originally wagered, dropped the envelope to the ground, and drove home.

He'd try again next week.

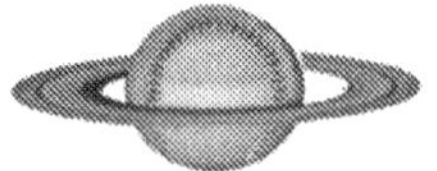

Paul Abbamondi reads and writes speculative fiction compulsively in New Jersey. No pets currently, but he's contemplating getting a tubby goldfish. His short stories have appeared in *Shimmer*, *Apex Digest*, and *Aberrant Dreams*, among other fine publications. By day, he works as an editor for a market research firm in New Jersey, and at night he plots to take over the world. He keeps a blog at http://wistfulwritings.blogspot.com, which is just as exciting as it sounds.

Ebonmadder's Run

Marge Simon

Bred from finest stock, ten billion eyes were on him
with countless sums invested in the outcome
of this, his final race: seven place to seven show.

Prancing to the dance of vidscan-shine,
(for after this he'd be sent home to stud--
to serve at leisure, such was his owner's promise)

nostrils flaring crimson, red in black
the colors of his silks, so given as his name,
Ebon strutted to his stall and took his space.

The gun went off, the gates released
as viewers on off-worlds upturned their seats,
to see him take the outside, slow and holding--

then gather speed, to overtake the leader
legs pumping, heart bursting he cleared the oval rail
with one ecstatic cry, dissolved into the void

which is *Continuendum*, the place beyond

the broadcast sector, a forbidden zone
where life meets instantaneous combustion.

At first, there was confusion in the viewing population;
yet in time, they concluded it was typical of homo sapiens
to destroy an opportunity for freedom.

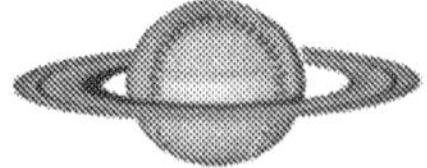

Marge Ballif Simon freelances as a writer-poet-illustrator for genre and mainstream publications. She has three collections coming out in 2007: *Vectors: A Week in the Death of a Planet* with Charlee Jacob (Dark Regions Press), *Like Birds in the Rain* (Sam's Dot Publishing) and *Night Smoke* with Bruce Boston (Kelp Queen Publications). Marge currently serves as editor of *Star*Line.*

"Ebonmadder's Run" first appeared in *Space & Time*, Spring 2000.

Somewhere, the Sun Is Shining

Jo L. Gerrard

The ball hovered in front of Timmons, poised at the precise mid-point of his strike zone. He twisted his hands on the tape wrapped around his light aluminum bat, palms sweaty beneath his synth-leather gloves. The sensor in the tip of his bat, hooked to the breakaway cable in his wrist, sent an electrical charge down his nerves, urging his muscles to swing.

But the pitch was *too* perfect, the ball an easy hit out of the station's park, into the darkness between the blurry stars visible through the roof. The bot-umpire behind him beeped once. Timmons didn't move. His eyes didn't leave the ball. The pitcher had programmed a twist, he was certain, the ball prepared to levitate or drop the moment his bat moved.

Three and two on the pitch, three on base. Sweat ran along the outside edge of Timmons' eye. The gathered space workers, depending on their loyalties, chanted his name or catcalled. The umpire gave a second warning beep. Five seconds to decide.

Eyes locked on the target, willing his bat to send the ball to the stars beyond, Timmons swung.

Jo Gerrard has been writing almost as long as she can remember. She has been published in *The Harrow*, *Astropoetica*, *Word Riot*, *remark*, and an upcoming issue of *Star*Line*.

Stealing for the Record

Robert Frazier

Lank and easy in his bones,
the mind-reader drifts off second
and sidesteps into his lead.
One out; he's confident of his advantage.
He sets his feet, scuffs the dirt for a hold,
spreads haunches, and crouches down:
knees bent, butt back, head forward.
For a moment the runner remembers another life,
sneaking comic books from the local drug store
and knowing when the soda jerk would check on him,
knowing from the color of the man's thoughts.
Now his arms seem to scissor out to bat wings,
sensing the ether for something mystical,
some plane of least resistance.
Sidestepping twice more towards third,
he lets the invisible chord that
binds him to the bag unwind and stretch,
and he waits to be snapped back in a blur.

As he's poised on an exact balance point,
animal hunger rises in the runner's throat

along with the acids of tension and gut fear.
His mind darts toward home, toward the dugout,
toward the coach's head at third.
Back to the fastball hurler.
The power of concentration burns
through his veins like a hundred dollar poison.
The shortstop adjusts.
He reads them again to assure himself
that all systems are green.
He awaits cryptic signs.

The pitcher begins his move,
commits in his mind
to make the pitch toward home plate.
The runner pivots and digs and accelerates
until his legs churn like egg beaters,
making clods of dirt spit behind him.
Time seems to balloon out like those seconds
when a driver loses control of a speeding car,
when he sees his life narrowed before him
into a long shining tunnel.
The slide is smooth, almost unnecessary.
The throw is on the button, but way late.
He rises easily to brush off while
tides of inertia shift in his plumbing.
Perhaps the cheers rise above him like startled birds.

Perhaps the benches will empty when
a long fly sends him in.
Perhaps memories of super heroes
warm his head with legend.

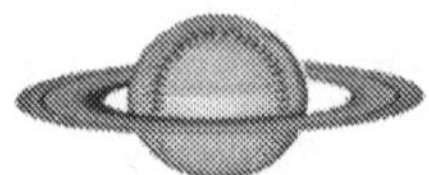

Robert Frazier lives on Nantucket Island and paints as a member of the Artists' Association of Nantucket. He is the author of eight books of poetry, and a three-time winner of the Rhysling Award for poetry. His books include *Co-Orbital Moons*, *Perception Barriers*, and *The Daily Chernobyl.* Recent works have appeared in *Asimov's Science Fiction* and *The Magazine of Fantasy & Science Fiction.* His collaborative poem with Bruce Boston "Chronicles of the Mutant Rain Forest" received first place in the 2006 *Locus Magazine* Online Poetry Poll for "Best All-Time Science Fiction, Fantasy, or Horror Poem." His most recent book is *The Art Colony on Nantucket: Sixty Years of Contemporary Art* (The AAN Press). For more information, visit http://en.wikipedia.org/wiki/Robert_Frazier.

"Stealing for the Record" first appeared in *Isaac Asimov's Science Fiction Magazine*, August 1990.

Perpetual Check

E.C. Myers

3:57 AM.

Aidan closed his eyes and felt the familiar stab of nausea as he was pulled from his apartment. A moment later he opened his eyes onto an old-fashioned sitting room. The Lady sat at her inlaid mahogany chessboard, its Staunton chess pieces already scattered in play. She nodded in greeting and he took the empty seat across from her, still warm from her previous opponent. She was playing white. She was always white.

"I missed you last week," she said. She pressed the old analog timer beside the board. "Your move." Ticking filled the room.

"I fell asleep," Aidan apologized. He peeked at her face while he examined the board. Flickering gaslight showed that she remained unchanged, as lovely as the first time he had been called to her table so many years ago.

The players who had taken their turns in the minutes before him hadn't left much to work with; a black onyx army of defeated pieces flanked the board. Aidan sighed. He jumped a pawn up a square then punched the timer. It was a wasted move, but he needed more time to form a strategy. He needed more time.

"This isn't exactly fair," he said, almost immediately wishing he could take the words back. The Lady knew all about unfairness. How many people faced her each night, moving only a few pieces in their turns?

"I won my last tournament," he said quickly. "I qualified as Candidate Master." He had dedicated his life to the game--to her. "I'm getting better all the time."

She smiled. Her hand darted to the board, moved a knight, and took his pawn in one smooth movement. His clock resumed ticking.

Aidan's father had given him a chess set for his seventh birthday. Shortly afterward, when Aidan stayed up late studying playbooks, he found himself facing the Lady, hopelessly infatuated. She was in her early twenties, then and always. Though he was much older than her now, he still loved her. She was the only woman he had ever loved.

"Time's almost up," she said. Aidan nudged a rook over to threaten the white queen. She raised her eyebrows then captured his rook with her queen. "Check."

His king dodged imminent danger and Aidan stopped the timer with only three seconds remaining.

"Have you ever lost?" he asked. The Lady always allowed him one question, but he had never asked her this--he thought that he might not have many more chances. He used to wonder if she was testing him and the other players who were each given a minute to play against her each week. He had slowly come to realize that it must be she who was being tested.

She maneuvered her own rook, setting him up for checkmate in two. He positioned a bishop to retaliate, to stall the inevitable, knowing he had no chance. Knowing he had failed her.

"Check." His last second ticked away.

"I lose every night," she said.

3:58 AM.

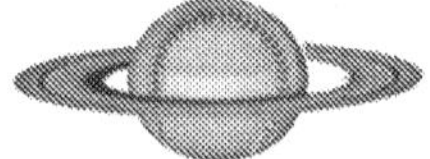

E.C. Myers lives in Manhattan, where he struggles to stay awake in the city that never sleeps. The results of his self-imposed sleep deprivation have appeared in a number of publications, including *flashquake*, *Fictitious Force*, and *From the Asylum.* He is a graduate of the Clarion West Writers Workshop and an active participant in the writing groups Altered Fluid and Fangs of God. More information about him and his work can be found at his website, http://www.ecmyers.net.

Riding to Faery

(after Anne Sexton)

C. A. Gardner

I'm hitching my horse's reins
to the post of the Fields Unknown.
This post is carved like a spiraling horn
and there is nothing but dust
in prints that hardened fast.
"Through the veil," I whisper in delight,
for the calluses that formed all fell
first formed then fell--
leaving my fingers free for the keyboard.
And words drumming through my tongue and ears like
fine needles tinkling shards of jagged glassware.
I leave my horse by the maple post
and wander among the tall grasses.
"Come to me!" Oberon calls and soon
I part weeds and we crouch on the cliff
with a board--carved from the rock--
of chess between us.
He takes my queen.
I outsmart him because I have surrounded his king.
He grins as he displays three queens.

The triple goddess has entered the game
but I smile for I knew it
seeing the horns atop his head
from the moment we started to play.
As his queens move on my pieces
and I whistle in glee at my clever trap,
he grins beneath antlers,
the baring of his teeth like points of bone-tipped spears
that dance and chatter,
white keys barbed and shaped with the power words,
naming the Slip-Veil between the two worlds.
Now I stand, and Oberon stands
the queens stand. My words stand.
The tall grasses waver and stand.

Affectionate horned man,
I with the gift of the clever,
need you with your grin of white words,
with your queens, your grasses, your unknown fields,
land fertile with magical lies.

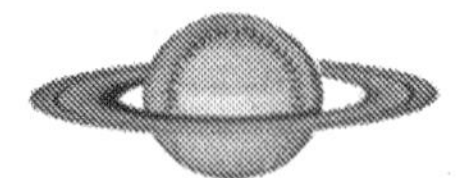

With master's degrees in English and library science, **C. A. Gardner** has been the editor at a private maritime museum and currently serves as cataloger for a public library. Thus far, 20 stories, 120 poems, 32 drawings and photographs, and 24 of her nonfiction pieces have been published in venues such as *Abyss & Apex*, *The Doom of Camelot*, *The Leading Edge*, *Legends of the Pendragon*, *Strange Horizons*, and *Talebones.* In 2004, Gardner attended the Clarion West Writers Workshop. For more information, visit http://www.gardnercastle.com.

"Riding to Faery" first appeared in *Mythic Delirium*, Winter/Spring 2002.

Running for Life

Brenta Blevins

"Why are you on this team?" Coach Salem, the new varsity cross country coach, towered above Mindy. With the late October afternoon sunshine behind her, the woman stood silhouetted like a malevolent shadow.

"I joined to, uh, run," Mindy stammered. She'd joined the team for one reason: practice was better than going home to three generations in a cramped trailer. At least the other girls couldn't overhear the Coach's criticisms as they ran laps around the track.

More than ever, Mindy missed the previous coach. Amy had hugged her, told her she'd done a good job, even though she always came in last. Coach Salem told everyone, even Susie Lee, who ran like a rabbit and was being pursued by college recruiters, to work harder.

"I want a reason by the end of practice or you're off the team." Coach Salem had a strange accent. None of the girls dared ask where she'd lived before.

"But—" If Mindy didn't run, she'd have to babysit her little brother.

"Running is about facing fear—worries of injury or the shame of finishing last, wondering if your legs will stop or if your lungs can squeeze in any more air. You girls have had it easy. I've run in snow and crossed rivers at meets."

No wonder Janiece called the coach a witch. Mindy counted the construction paper black cats taped to the library windows.

"I've marked a new course through the woods with obstacles to challenge you to go faster and farther."

Mindy glanced at the pine forest behind the school. Mrs. Hall, the office secretary, had once told her about two students she'd thought were truant, but had been found dead in the woods. She'd confided she thought the woods were now haunted.

"You'll run alone while the girls do laps." Coach Salem raised her voice. The sinking sun turned pumpkin orange. "If you think this is too hard, you can quit now."

Mindy shook her head.

"Go!" The Coach clicked her stopwatch.

Mindy headed down the course, over the peach clay path into the pine trees. In the dark woods, she strained to see ghosts to avoid and course flags to follow.

As her muscles grew warm, her pace evened and her thoughts flowed with her strides, creating a rhythm, as opinions, ideas, and her Spanish homework ran through her mind.

Correr. To run. *Corro.* I run. I hope I don't end up working late every night like my mother, then living with her and my own children in the same trailer.

Corremos. We run. Mindy hoped she wouldn't develop her grandmother's diabetes. Veering, Mindy spotted a fluorescent orange flag twisting in the breeze and turned left through an even thicker grove of pines, so dark the needles seemed black. Mindy had already run further than she had at previous practices. Her breathing was so heavy she sounded like the victim in a horror movie. Why had Coach made her, the slowest runner, run alone so late? She'd never finish before nightfall. She'd get lost.

As Mindy ran past, a warty green mask with red eyes swiveled on a tree branch. Did the Coach think that would scare her? She heard rustling behind her, glanced back, and her eyes focused on a shadow separating from the tree. She shrieked and her feet tangled, sending her slamming into the dirt.

The "mask" rose, moving toward her. Not walking. Slithering—maybe. Black leg after leg unfolded, rolling through the inky shadows toward Mindy. The red eyes twinkled as they stared back at her.

Cold wind whistled through the pine needles. No one could hear her scream out here. Mindy shivered as if she'd run through snow. She scrambled, wondering which way to escape. Would continuing on be the fastest way back to school? Surely, she was at least halfway along the path. She sprinted away, glanced over her shoulder and saw the shadow pursuing. She slid in rust-colored pine needles and plunged to the hard clay.

The thing glided toward her.

Mindy bolted. How far away was the school? Mindy's lungs felt like they'd burst into flames. Her steps staggered as she kept turning to see behind.

She felt the trail under her feet more than she could see it. Hounding her, the thing snuffled, snorted with an inhuman mouth, and she felt its breath as icy gusts on her back. Every glance behind her confirmed she couldn't outrun it.

Mindy glimpsed a light twinkling through the trees in the distance, like a star on the horizon. Remembering her childhood habit, she made a wish on the star. She focused ahead, her stride lengthening, growing smooth as she pushed on. The safety of the light beckoned.

Coach wanted her to quit. That's why she'd summoned the thing, but Mindy wouldn't give her the satisfaction. She ran on, refusing to acknowledge the thing behind. She wanted to improve, to grow into a confident, healthy, strong athlete. Her breathing evened, grew controlled.

Her feet now glided over a path made invisible by nightfall. She might never become an Olympian, nor be recruited by a college, but running was about more than just avoiding the family's trailer after school. Running helped her grow stronger, healthier, braver. The light grew larger, brighter.

Mindy emerged from the woods and continued toward the parking lot's security lamp. Her mother waited by the car.

Gasping, Mindy bent, placing her raw hands on her dirty knees.

Coach Salem approached. "Now, what's your philosophy of running?"

Mindy sucked in air. She turned, but saw behind only the pines swaying in the night wind. "It's better to have a goal to run toward than to be merely running away."

The Coach clicked the stopwatch. "This was your best time this season."

Mindy's mom handed her a towel. "Coach says you and your team might be the first to make State this year. Did you have a good practice?"

"I did." Mindy grinned. And the Coach did likewise. "Thanks."

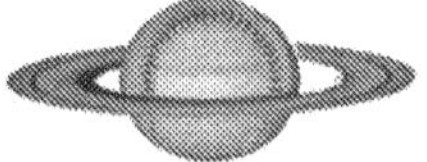

Brenta Blevins lives in the Appalachian Mountains, where she enjoys hiking with her husband. A graduate of Virginia Tech, Brenta has written audio dramas that have been produced for public radio and non-fiction that has been published in *Strange Horizons*.

Leaves

James S. Dorr

She ran like leaves spinning
through bat filled alleys,
through shadows tabbied
in brown and auburn
by distant neon,
to break to the meadows,
the wood beyond them,
the stars' fitful winking out
at the dawn's first glow.
Panting, she sought the earth,
leaf-loam protecting
root tunnels of ancient trees
gnarled in the daytime's light
but, under, opening
to marble slabbed coolness,
to sleep and, yes, lie in hope
of a next moonrise.
She had been a runner --
her life ticked in seconds
off timekeepers' stopwatches,
counting the meters from starting blocks,

end tapes,
and, always, leaves falling,
rivals behind her,
sweat gushing from open pores.
Now death's blood pounded
through calloused veins, yet,
even as in life she had strived
ever for new marks
so, in her new undeath, she,
mocking the sun's sprint from pre-dawn
to full light,
sought still to post records.

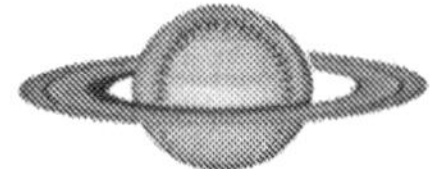

James Dorr's new book, *Darker Loves: Tales of Mystery and Regret*, is due out from Dark Regions Press as a companion to his current fiction and poetry collection, *Strange Mistresses: Tales of Wonder and Romance* (Dark Regions, 2001). Other recent poetry has appeared in *Star*Line*, *Doorways*, *The Vile Vineyard*, *Baltimore 40 Program Book*, *Dwarf Stars*, and *Bondage: Tales of Obsession*. Indiana resident Dorr is a member of the Science Fiction Poetry Association and a multi-time Rhysling finalist as well as an active member of SFWA and HWA.

"Leaves" first appeared in *The Magazine of Speculative Poetry*, Autumn 1997.

The Empress of the Dragon

Adam Nakama

"Let's go ride the Dragon," Mei would say to Chonglei, and his face would immediately scowl—she'd *have* to call him a pickled plum, pinch his cheeks, and that only made him scowl worse. But her enthusiasm eventually won out over her little brother, and so soon they were racing to the top, climbing up shifting gears, scrabbling over pulsing pistons, leaping between swooping pendulums as they creaked back and forth. Mei was never sure whether she was laughing or screaming when she rode the screeching chains rushing to the top.

"Hold on," she'd yell back to Chonglei, "hold on tight!" and right before they hit the top where the chain would turn over the toothed pulley—leaving her hands mangled if she stayed—she would let go and fly, letting the momentum carry her up, up, up, arms outstretched, reaching for the next bar or ledge. She always grabbed it, though her heart was always pounding too.

Very seldom did she fail to beat her brother. She would catch her breath waiting for him in the neck, so that she'd appear to have expended no effort in the dangerous rush to the top. He'd scowl again, frustrated, when he met her there, but Mei would only laugh and take his hand and lead him into the head. From there they could see the land for many li around, the hills of Kwei-lin stretching out like the unfurling coils of a dragon swimming, while the metal man the children rode lumbered between them.

"I can't believe father built this," Mei would say, her breathlessness catching up with her.

"Father never wanted you," Chonglei would mutter, or something like it, barely audible over the clanking of the clockwork. But Mei would not let it bother her. Up here, the world unfolded before her and she was its Empress. Beautiful, all.

When her brother got older, a teenager, and invited all his friends, riding the Dragon transformed from a game into a kind of sport, a race to the top by a handful of kids. Although her brother's friends were often stronger than her, Mei was still faster and always beat them. Nobody understood the clockwork man like she did; nobody else knew of its secret valves and chambers, cutting through the circuitous clockwork. Nobody else—not even her father, she thought—had seen what lay inside them.

Word of this challenge spread, and from provinces across the Middle Kingdom came boys, and then men to climb the clockwork giant. Mei was no longer allowed to ride. Her father forbade her on the grounds that she should learn the duties of a young woman preparing to marry. And the older men riding the Dragon did not want the presence of a girl tainting their sport.

She did not regret this. She knew that she would be forbidden some day. She simply did not let it stop her. Although she loved showing that she could beat those boys, it was not for camaraderie or competition that she climbed up through the clockwork man.

So she rode it in the twilight of morning, climbing nimbly

amongst the push and pull of the living machine, and watched the sun rise over the hills through his lofty eyes.

She never married. Men scurried around the both of them; her brother kept her in his household, "for the children loved their energetic aunt so." And as her father passed into senescence, Mei and the clockwork man kept one another company through the long Middle Kingdom dawns, quiet except the shifting of machinery. With him, she remained an Empress, waiting for the regular ascent of Heaven from the height of her unconquered throne.

Adam Nakama is currently finishing undergraduate studies at Worcester Polytechnic Institute, with majors in mathematics and literature, and recently completed a thesis on hypertext literature which won the 2007 Provost's Award for Major Qualifying Projects. You can read the results at http://www.storynouveau.com/mqp. He is also slated for publication in the *Field Guide to Surreal Botany* and *Scifaikuest*. In addition to writing, Adam designs and participates in Alternate Reality Games and dances tango. You can visit him at http://elenuial.livejournal.com.

Less Than Perfect

Todd Wheeler

Oh yeah, you gotta be perfect on *The Dare*, 'cause the best of the best in all the world will show you up for a chump if you're not. Reigning champ, Diego Paz, seven weeks running, mastered them all. A math wiz and polyglot, Kung-Fu beast and tri-ath god, half the world's favorite son, the other half wants to see him undone.

Along comes the spider, Eleanor Mack, acrobat and kayak queen. Jet black hair streaked with red. Muscles taut, the slammin' poet, she kicked down the doors and hit her spot on the stage and whispered, soft yet shot through with steel:

"I dare you ..."

Uh-huh, you better bring your "A" game on *The Dare* 'cause the freaky AI brooks no fault. In its aluminum drum is the sum of all experts, memorized facts and subjectives. Fast as a dick on a trick, no foolin' it, 'cause that thing knows if you're fraudulent.

They're squaring up with whisks and knives 'cause Eleanor threw it down, Iron-Chef style, gotta make a meringue, not lemon but lime. Diego is bang and flash, smirk on his face as he whips and whacks, while Eleanor works focused. She perspires, juggling eggs, and the audience thinks she is one-and-done 'cause the drop of sweat on her lip drips right into the bowl! Oh, but she smiles, that tear of salt purposed, part of the flan-plan. She flames the peaks with twirling torches.

Two slices of pie delivered on glass. The AI takes them in with syringes, analyzing with molecular tongue. That cartoon of a robot huffs and yumms and belches, and rolling up them googly yellow eyes, spits out the verdict: a tie.

Whoa, Nellie! What's this? Sponsors hard up for ratings? The world is debating, is the game fixed? Or a fault in the coding? 'Cause how could they both be perfect?

But, the ruling stands and the following week it's put to the man. Diego sneers while half the world jeers and the other half cheers, and lookin' at Eleanor like a hungry mutt, he sputters out the gritted dare:

"Guitars of air."

Dressed in glitter and platform shoes, Diego throws a curve and legislates the bass majestic, channeling Bootsy's funkadelic. No fool, Eleanor keeps with the heat and beguiles like Jimi's Voodoo child. Barefoot, in a leather dress slit to the hip, she bumps and grinds, now fast, now sublime, and even Diego looks surprised.

That creepy bot shudders and jumps, potato-head ears spinnin', buck-tooth mouth grinnin', it makes its final decision: a tie.

"No!" they scream around the planet. But, dammit, the show goes on. Week after week, Diego Paz and Eleanor Mack perform their tricks, layin' bricks, inserting stents, levitating elephants. And the damn AI with a lazy eye, wheezes, teases: a tie.

So there on stage, woman and man stand, a centimeter between breast and chest. Diego is average height, she's not slight, and their sight is lasered on each other. Lids wide open, eyeballs bare, 'cause the dare is to stare and stare and stare.

The audience too, gnawing fists, looks and looks so as not to miss, 'cause in this test, surely one must be the best. They can't possibly both be perfect.

Their muscles twitch with the heat of their breath on their faces. Eleanor and Diego, depth of their perception traces pupil and iris, like the stillness of night skies, mesmerized. Diego sweats, red face baking, and Eleanor starts shaking, and around the world they can't bear it. One must win they think. The camera moves in on the salty drop that beads up on his lip and with the tip of her tongue she licks that drip and she moans.

Diego blinks.

Oh yeah, you gotta be perfect on *The Dare*, 'cause the best of the best in all the world will show you up for a chump if you're not. Reigning champ, Eleanor Mack, ten weeks running, mastered them all. Perspired, she retired, undefeated, to a little villa on the coast. She and Diego doing their best to raise a brood of kids they love. Even if none of them are perfect.

Todd Wheeler is a writer of speculative fiction. His work has been published in several online and print magazines, including *Atomjack*. When not writing, he stays busy as a stay-at-home dad, which is just as satisfying and pays about the same. For more information, visit him at http://todd-wheeler.com or http://todd-wheeler.blogspot.com.

Inland Sea

Beth Langford

At first she cuts maps into the uneven surface of the ice. She skates slowly, tentatively, the way she must have done when she was first learning: she pushes her toes apart and brings them back together to carve out the shapes of bubbles, each one floating her a little further forward. Behind her an archipelago of them stretches out, stretches far.

The ice is tinted green. The colour's due to minerals or pollutants or a bit of both, I'm not sure, but the landscape is made of milky jade streams. They curve and bend: knees and elbows. They join together in the bottom of this little valley, here where Erin unfreezes her own slow bones. Spreads out her arms. Turns carefully. Turns again until she stumbles and her toe pick jams on a bump. I hold my breath, but she whoops and catches herself and looks back at me.

I smile. I'm tightening my scarf. The wind thinks it's a big old bear, taking swipes at my cold face. Maybe the blushes in my cheeks look like fish under ice. Maybe it's not me it's after at all. Deep down the rock holds the dark outlines of beings that flourished in a kinder age. This was an inland sea.

And the ice, too, is teeming. It holds a hawk's telltale shadow spun sideways, the sharp click of goats' hooves. The wind, that grizzly, knocks wolves' howls out of it like bees from a hive.

Erin's at the toes of the mountain—those big, lumpy digits made by stream deltas, the crevices between them so narrow she glides in one foot in front of the other, resting her hand on rock, on snow. The snow that is absence: no tracks. (When we first found this place, it had been packed down with them: delicate crows' feet, cloven hooves, and something else, heavier and unsettling.) She glides back out into the sort-of rink in the valley basin. "I'm going to do a double salchow," she shouts.

"Careful," I say. "Are you sure the ice is even enough?" I sound like her robot Joshua, going off about preventable injuries. Last time he did that I tried to be clever: "All injuries are preventable, by definition, aren't they? Just avoid doing anything." He did the "does not compute" routine he does when he doesn't want to humour me.

I'm not too worried. Back when the lakes used to freeze downmountain, reliably anyway, I remember her landing a triple. Or maybe it wasn't a salchow but a lutz, or an axel—I only know the names. I remember how pleased she looked. (Blood-and-bones Josh had missed it, so she made a second attempt, but landed two-footed.) I think my friends went skating often, back then, just for fun. Not me—I was never any good.

The sun comes out and Erin's warming up like the air, gliding backwards—impressively—over the ice's shallow wounds and markings, gliding faster. I notice the valley filling up. Children in bright blue breathers drop a puck and watch it slide downstream over the unfair ice. Below us a bus marked Columbia Tourist Tours is stopped at the end of a runaway lane, inexplicably, as if there were something to see there.

Now Erin is doing crossovers, her hands out. She skates wide ovals—so many I almost forget she's going to jump. That's until she puts her foot out (the children are watching) and takes off—spins tightly, twice, perfect. This all in one breath of mine. I watch as she sets down, an honorary heron, one foot. Then the other and she stumbles. I catch my breath and shoot out an ineffectual hand as she wobbles—this graceful too, but scary—and falls down hands-first.

I see her shake her head a little. "I hit water," she says. "Melting."

"Are you alright?" My breather vibrates.

"I'm alright," she shouts into the quiet and gets up creakily, tentatively, like the first chunk of ice breaking off in spring melt. When she's up, a small family of skaters cheers. She smiles, embarrassed.

I wait until no one's paying attention any longer to go to her. Walking across the ice I notice how scuffed it is, how hard and white all the blades have made it. There are no more shadows in it, no more howlers, nor swimmers, no more walking worms, nor eagles, nor elk.

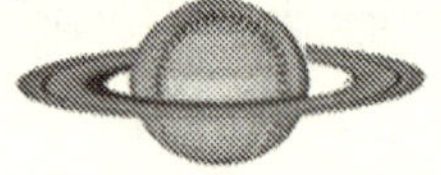

Beth Langford recently graduated from university with a degree in zoology. She lives in Vancouver with several unbalanced hanging plants and an antisocial cactus. Her flash fiction has appeared in *A Field Guide to Surreal Botany*, *Aoife's Kiss*, and *Kaleidotrope*.

Approaching Europa

Deborah P Kolodji

Flawless virgin ice,
untouched by a single blade.
twenty-one axel
        vigesimal toe loop…

She looks through the porthole
with a figure skater's eyes.

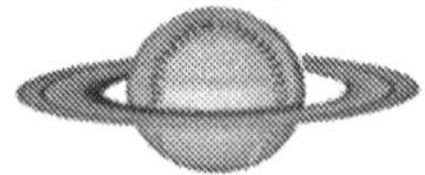

Deborah P Kolodji is the president of the Science Fiction Poetry Association and a member of the Haiku Society of America. She is the editor of *Amaze: The Cinquain Journal*, and has published four chapbooks of poetry. Her work has appeared in *Strange Horizons*, *Modern Haiku*, *Raven Electrick*, *Frogpond*, *Dreams and Nightmares*, *bottle rockets*, *Tales of the Unanticipated*, and *Chicken Soup for the Dieter's Soul*, among many other publications.

Hang Twenty

Jude-Marie Green

His doctors lie to the media, on my orders. It is not a skin disease.

The best waves run under the full moon. A creature of my nature feels the pull of the tides. They surge like blood through my veins. Others of my kind lope through ancient forests in the old country; in this new country, the surf competitions, offer the same wild release.

Dog-surfing, it's called, or hang twenty: one person and one dog riding a board. The competition is new but dogs and people have played this sport together since Hawaii and the first surfboards.

I park my top-down convertible on the street. The competition will take place in the sand beach ten yards away. I watch the sun gleam on the waves. Seagulls circle overhead, damnable vermin. Sometimes the birds provide sport for me and my pack. They always underestimate how far we can leap.

My pack saunters to me, surrounds my car. They ignore the new member I've brought, the lupine curled up on the shotgun seat. I count and acknowledge them all: four nephews, three nieces, my mate. If we were alone we'd be tussling and kissing. Lack of privacy and eyes of strangers call for some subtleness. I murmur each name as I glance at them.

Cassidy is most-junior and most-brash.

"Why'd you bring him?" he growls. The fear in his voice tickles my nostrils.

I run my fingernails across his shoulders and smile. "He's good. Better than you," I say.

Cassidy snarls and circles around my new acquisition. On first glance it looks like a black dog, scrawny and flea-bitten. On second glance the muscles are apparent, the feral eyes gleam with blood-lust, the red lips pull back from wolf-teeth.

Cassidy blows a snort at the new wolf and shakes his head. "I won't share a board with that thing," he declares.

"But I will," I say. "It's not a threesome." I keep my eyes on the new one, not sparing a glance at Cassidy. The boy takes the snub and stumbles back from me.

The loudspeaker blares something incomprehensible. We walk towards our surfboards, planted in an upright semicircle. A moon-crescent. Two of my nieces, one of my nephews turn for this day's events. The pack shelters them from prying eyes.

I stand next to my board with the new one at my feet and wait for my number to be called.

My mate sidles up next to me, not touching. Philippe knows that a thrill of distance between bare skin makes the blood race ever hotter. He never fails to excite me. My breath catches.

"Bella," he murmurs, an endearment, not my name. "Who is he?" His tone is reasonable and disinterested. I match his nonchalance as I tell him.

He sucks in a gasp, then asks, "Have you lost your mind?" Philippe can turn in an instant. I need to stop him. I place my hand on his wrist.

"He sings," I say. My pack shuffles. Our singing is lackluster, toneless. They do not accept the new one, not yet, but they won't kill him now.

"We'll tell them he's in Africa. Dubai. We have wolves there."

I plop him down on the front of the board and paddle out beyond the first wave break. He's unsure, unsteady, but not frightened. He does not take to his feet even when I turn the board and sit up.

I count for a good wave. Three curls that peter out, one that is cross-riffed, one that is good. I wait for the good one then paddle in advance of it, gaining speed as the water humps up under the board.

I stand, place my feet, push the board onto the wave.

The wolf stands and his mouth hangs open, his tongue out.

The wave breaks under us, behind us. The thrill drenches me as much as the salt spray. My breath ratchets and I fling my arms out for balance, bending at the knees a bit, the wave is curling over us.

The wolf stands on his hind legs, exposing his belly. His tail is not curled over his balls: he is not afraid.

He howls. His silky black hair streams back and tickles my legs. He howls as loud as the pounding ocean. My hair streams, cutting into the wave wall itself. I howl.

The wave is about to spit us out, a successful ride, when he falls off. He tries to plant his four paws on the board, overbalances, lurches forward and rolls into the water.

I curse even as I dive off the board after him.

When last I visited his private zoo, to woo his home-grown wolves, I'd found him waiting. When I nipped him, changed him, I promised he'd suffer no harm. When the moon came for him, I called his name to bring him into my pack.

"Michael."

At the end of the long day, I haven't won. No one of my pack has. The domesticated dogs—the jack russell, the german shepherd, the lab, the tame pets that grovel for a human master's approval, they offer the best tricks.

Cassidy does not take defeat well. He eyes the dogs and their humans. "I'm hungry," he announces. "We should feast."

It's a question awaiting the slightest agreement from me. Our fire pit could roast food better than hotdogs, tastier than barbeque ribs. My eyes narrow and I feel the wild pulse just under my skin.

But no. The surf is enough for today.

My pack gathers round me as the night comes on and we do not care. We've surfed. We eat. We howl.

The moon, full and bloody, rises. Each strand of my hair tingles. My new pet's fur stands on end. He puts his snout in the air and lets go of the wild in his soul. We sing together. My pack joins the song.

We love the way he howls.

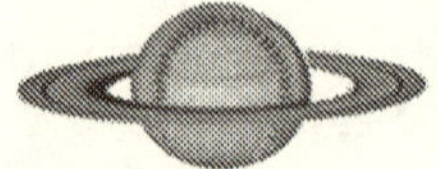

Jude-Marie Green lives in Southern California and does not surf. She lives with books, birds, and cats, and writes genre fiction that has been published in *Say*, *Abyss & Apex*, and *Ideomancer*, as well as in the anthologies *Visual Journeys* and *Legends of the Mountain State*.

Star Boarding

Marcie Lynn Tentchoff

We used to race in silence,
the only sound the blood
that pounded through our veins.

We strove for records,
all alone against a backdrop
of the gem-encrusted night.

Strapped astride our starboards,
in our armored, heat resistant,
vacuum-tested suits,

Our star sails open, mirrored,
set to take the smallest bits of light,
transforming them to speed,

We steered for glory, edging
ever closer to the stars that gave
us power, to stars that held our fate.

And then we left it, left the racing,

left the silence, left the loneliness
behind, for newer folk to claim.

We see them watch us, there, out of
the corners of their eyes. We know
they think we lost our nerve.

Someday they will learn better,
out there, by some star, they'll face
the choice we each have made.

Shall they press closer, thieve
that extra bit of power from a sun,
and turn into the energy they court?

Shall they turn to light, to heat,
to flowing, never-ending speed,
out amidst the emptiness of space?

Or walk away, and leave the stars
up in the sky, untouchable,
unjoinable, and dim.

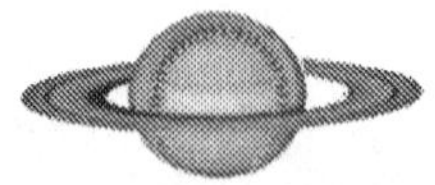

Marcie Lynn Tentchoff is an Aurora Award winning poet/writer from the west coast of Canada, where she lives in the middle of a rainforest with her family and various animals, both invited and not. She's written poems and stories that have appeared in such magazines as *On Spec*, *Weird Tales*, *Dreams and Nightmares*, *Talebones*, and *Illumen*, as well as in various anthologies.

Prey

Paul L. Bates

I knew he was a god from the moment I found him, but which one remained uncertain. He was not above accepting my help, and he made no claims to anything. I knew at once that he was neither the bombastic God of Abundance, nor the bellicose God of War. There was no cleverness or trickery in his manner of speaking, ruling out the possibility that he was the God of Reason. He was too well fed and self contained to be the God of Mercy. His moods had no effect whatever upon the weather, so I knew that he was not the Stormbringer. But I am getting far ahead of myself.

I found him sitting on the end of a park bench, watching the sun rise above the city towers. He looked up and saw me for what I was, a hunter.

"Another moment for your collection," he said quietly, and smiled.

I said nothing and sat down respectfully at the opposite end of the bench, leaving a wide space between us. The sky was still the deepest possible shade of velvet night blue with only a line of crimson sizzling at the jagged edge of the world, where the skyline fell far short of heaven, yet I could see his face as clearly as if it were illuminated by the full moon.

"You're a long way from home," I said after a while.

He laughed and said, "Not really."

I drew a silver flask from my breast pocket and slowly removed the cap. I took a swig of the smooth brandy, felt the sweet warmth gliding over my tongue and down my throat. Then, leaning toward him, I offered him the flask. He accepted my hospitality without deliberation and drank deeply enough that I was able to rule out a host of possible identities with that single gesture.

"An especially fine brandy," he commented.

I noticed that he was reluctant to return my flask. I offered him the cap and he graciously accepted it.

"Why this bench?" I asked.

"You really don't know, do you?"

"I surmise it has something to do with the view."

"The view is an illusion."

"All things are an illusion."

"Yes and no."

I turned back to watch the pink fading slowly to orange around the towers.

"They look like teeth to me," I said.

"They are. That is the Maw of Infinity. At least it is for the next few minutes."

"Ahh," I purred, understanding at last. "How long has it been?"

"I remember men after the deluge, when motherless children wore the skins of lesser brutes and fashioned words by moonlight huddling beneath the shelter of overhanging rocks, waiting for the lightning to set something ablaze."

I laughed aloud and he joined in.

"You pitied them."

"My folly," he admitted.

"You paid dearly for that sin."

He took another swig from the flask, and then offered it to me.

I declined and he nodded his thanks.

"How many of us have you collected?" he asked.

"I do not count—it seems disrespectful."

He looked back at me and his eyes burned another hole through my soul. I felt my entrails ravaged, my mind blasted, and my body shook like a sapling before a raging wind. Stars flashed by me like meteors, and I heard the buzzing of a thousand angry bees. I trembled for the better part of five minutes, as the perspiration sucked my shirt against my torso. The clanging of his medallion spinning to a stop beside me on the bench slats broke the spell.

For an instant I saw the sharp incisors bathed in a golden glow as he shot well past them, and then I watched the great orange fire ball rising languidly above the man-made cliffs at the edge of the sea.

When the spasms subsided, I picked up the medallion and placed it in my pocket where the flask had been.

I knew his name, but I would not speak it.

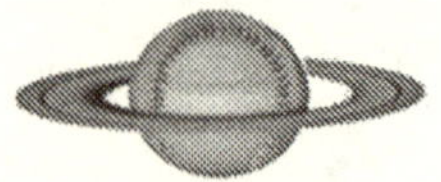

Paul L. Bates lives a life of astounding adventure, flies without the use of a cape, is lord to a host of fearsome clawed and fanged beings that remain docile as kittens around him. He is also plagued by recurring nightmares of being a construction estimator, spending tedious hours in a cramped office counting many odd things of which most people remain blessedly unaware. His novel, *Imprint*, was published in 2005. His short fiction can be found on occasion in such venues as *Zahir*, *Literal Latte* and *Lynx Eye*. A second novel, *Dreamer*, is scheduled for release in 2008.

The Tithing Hunt

Samantha Henderson

Tallyho and Tantivy,
the hounds have got the scent.
Fiddledum and fiddledee,
I see the fox ahead of me,
the horn is blowing merrily,
the Master is hell-bent.

Over fence and under tree,
the horses pound the ground.
Over stone and under sea,
the breeze is blowing over me,
the stallion strains beneath my knee—
I hear a dreadful sound.

Two by two and ten by ten,
the fox has gone to earth.
The dogs are tearing up the den,
I think that he's escaped, and then
a hand, an elbow bends again,
as if the ground gave birth.

Labyrinth and misfit maze,
his throat is bruised and torn.
We stand about him in a daze
and dimly dream of human ways.
I flinch and meet his desperate gaze,
and know that by the morn --

(grim December, merry May)
I'll pay the price of sin.
I'll flee the hounds until the day
the hunt shall find me anyway,
and for the pleasure of the Fae
will tear me from my skin.

Mare and stallion, filly, foal,
if gentleman or maid,
you'll ride and share the silver bowl
and never think to pay the toll
until the hounds shall rend your soul
and reckoning be paid.

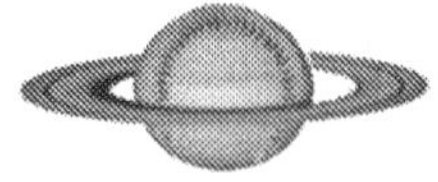

Samantha Henderson lives in Southern California with her family. Her poetry has been published in markets such as *Strange*

Horizons, *Weird Tales*, *Chizine*, *Dreams and Nightmares*, *Lone Star Stories*, *Abyss and Apex*, and *Ideomancer*. For more information, see her website at http://www.samanthahenderson.com.

The Football Phase

Connor Moran

"800-year-old wizards can not play college football!"

He just tilted his head a little. "Why not?" he asked.

"Graaah," I said, waving my hands at him. Before becoming live-in personal assistant to a wizard, I never thought I'd be in an argument like this. Now it seemed it happened every day. "First off, you'd have to be in college."

He blinked at me again. There was a quiver in space and then I was looking in the face of every stupid frat boy who'd ever shouted drunken come-ons at me back in school. I had to admit, he had the look down pat—from the shell necklace to the spiked-up hair. It was enough to make me long for his Harry Potter-inspired "Boy Wizard" phase.

"Change your look all you want, Garsalog, you're still not enrolled."

He looked distant for a moment. There was another quiver, then he grinned a big stupid frat-boy grin. "Are you sure?"

I took a deep breath, holding back the urge to tell him that he didn't have the physical capabilities. The last thing I needed was for him to punt or spike something. God save me from exuberant wizards.

I took a different tack. "If you show up out of nowhere and perform impossibly well, it's going to attract the wrong kind of attention. You don't want other wizards coming to take your power in a stadium full of people."

He just grinned at me again. I threw up my hands.

"Wizards!" I said.

I didn't go with him to the walk-on tryouts. College boys don't have personal assistants, I explained, and I was about ten years and twenty-five pounds beyond being able to pass as a bimbo girlfriend. I cut him off before he could suggest a mystical solution—after one overly memorable blind date I swore off glamours forever.

So I didn't see him play until he shouted me down from my room that night and excitedly pointed at the TV. It was a sports report on the local news. The announcer chattered excitedly about the mystery walk-on. Video showed a helmeted figure I could only assume was Garsalog tossing perfect spiral passes and outrunning the other players.

"Garsalog," I said. "What happened to staying below the radar?"

"I tried to hold back," he said. "I guess I didn't do it well enough."

I glared at him. He practically giggled.

"This is serious," I said. "Anyone could see this."

His face straightened up a little. "Now, now. I don't think many evil wizards are knowledgeable about college sports. And I know all of the players and coaches well enough. I don't think we need to worry about anything until the first scrimmages that are open to the public."

I rubbed my temples. "Whatever you say, Garsalog."

Over the next month the "to-read" pile next to my bed shrank and I got a lot better at crossword puzzles. Garsalog threw himself completely into his role as a college athlete—there was almost nothing for me to do. He even went to classes sometimes. I almost started to like the whole idea. Then one evening over dinner he declared that the first open scrimmage would be the next day.

"You'll love it," he said.

"I'm bringing my crossword puzzle," I said.

There were about fifty other people scattered about the bleachers, all absorbed in the game below. Though I could tell that Garsalog was holding himself back, I was surprised to find that he was quite fun to watch. When he cocked back his arm and fired a perfect pass some 50 yards down the field, I couldn't help but be impressed. I'd never seen him use magic to enhance his natural skills before.

I was so absorbed I didn't notice the strange man until it was almost too late.

He sat three rows below me. Even though the day was cloudless, he wore a yellow rain jacket over purple plaid pants. Where do you even get purple plaid pants? I should have spotted him right away, but I honestly didn't know what kind of people to expect at a college football scrimmage.

Then I heard him saying strange words, and I knew what was going on. I clenched my jaw. Too far away to warn Garsalog. I reached into my handbag and pulled out a small spray can. I shook it gently and tried to sneak up quietly behind the strange man. I felt like my every step on the metal bleachers could wake the dead. I stepped down to the row right behind him.

I held my breath, took two steps closer, then sprayed him with the can.

"Wha-aaaaargh!" he cried. I sprayed until the can was empty. He gasped. "What did you do?"

"Essence of wizardsbane," I said. "How's it taste?" It wouldn't hurt him, but he wouldn't be casting any spells. At least until he had a long shower.

Then I heard a gasp from the rest of the crowd. Garsalog had collapsed.

I swore. Another wizard, and I'd used up all my wizardsbane. I galloped down the bleachers, down the stairs and towards the entrance to the field. I blew past the security guard before he could move to stop me.

When I reached Garsalog, he was back on his feet. He stood a dozen yards from another man. They both had hands outstretched at each other. The coaches and players stood on the field, wide-eyed and useless. I looked around desperately for anything that could help. I saw the football, abandoned on the turf. "Garsalog," I said, then lunged for it and tossed it to him.

He snagged the ball, cocked it back, then planted a perfect spiral on the other wizard's chin. The other wizard collapsed.

I walked over and picked up the football, then carried it back to Garsalog. I planted it in his chest then leaned over to his ear.

"Next time you don't listen, I force-feed it to you."

Garsalog just smiled a sheepish smile.

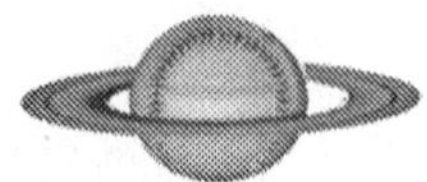

Connor Moran is a graduate of The Evergreen State College with an emphasis in creative writing. His comics and stories have appeared in *Alice Blue Review*, *Slightly West*, and the *Cooper Point Journal.* His comic, "The Angriest Rice Cooker in the World," along with other writing, appears at http://www.angriestricecooker.com. He lives in Olympia, Washington with his girlfriend, Sarah, and their cat, Nausicaa.

1967 NFC Championship Game Remembered After Awakening from Cryogenic Sleep

(for Bob Frazier)

Roger Dutcher

The memories surface slowly:
ice crystals sparkling,
blinding, shimmering together,
others melting and evaporating
in the new heat
of synapses firing after so long.
They say it is not unusual
to recall memories of cold first.
I remember the heat primarily.
And that all my relatives
were cheering for Dallas.
We were visiting Arizona and
I wanted it to be cold.
Christmas and football
were not meant for the heat,
at least not for a Midwest adolescent.
I watched the screen intently,

sweating, while my youthful heroes,
Starr, Kramer, Wood, and Brown,
fought not only Dallas,
but the elements they loved.
My relatives complained:
Green Bay has an unfair advantage,
you are used to the cold.
After the win,
my soul filled with wind and ice,
I went out to laugh
in a yard of stones,
longing to stoop,
make a snow ball
and hurl it through the desert heat
to hit the sun.

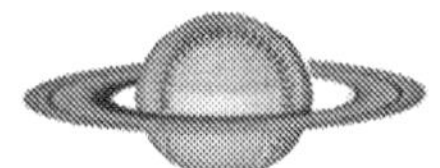

Roger Dutcher is the editor of *The Magazine of Speculative Poetry*, which he founded, with Mark Rich, in 1984. He also co-edits the poetry portion of online magazine *Strange Horizons.* His poetry has appeared in *Asimov's*, *Modern Haiku* and numerous other journals. His poem "Just Distance" won the Rhysling Award for best short poem of 2003.

"1967 NFC Championship Game..." first appeared in *Isaac Asimov's SF Magazine*, April 1991.

Blackthorn Darts

Amanda M. Hayes

It was a question, so Aemil said, of craftsmanship. All else was secondary to cutting the curse, and that was not only a matter of making clean incisions—you had to pierce your palm with the needle and leave it there for a night. You had to rub salt in before and while you worked so that the pain would be *there*, easy to reach, easy to carve into the darts for someone else to know. The fresh wounds on young tribal hands and knots of scar on old told Jense that this secret was widespread.

Fine: he baptized his needle appropriately. The salt he left alone; his cursing didn't need that kind of pain.

He worked through the whispers in his mind. All the voices were variants of his own, and they reminded him that the contest was just that, only sport with true harm forbidden. The harvest game determined who had the clever will to master the blackthorn darts. Who could be strikers and keep them all safe and hidden. Six years' stolen and broken-tipped practice thorns lay under Jense's bed as tribute to that dream—

You'll be burned, said the whispers. *You'll be killed.*

None of it had power over the memory of his sister torn and bare and dead, driven into soft loam by the boy who stood over her and buckled his belt again; the stab of pain in Jense's shoulder from a dart whose cuttings said *Silence.*

Jense let furious tears fill his etchings, and there was salt enough.

The day began with yells and clapping for all of them. The tang of snakes roasting promised a rare feast later. Their magi held up the chains of agates the winners would wear. Across the clearing, Quicevit smiled. He was narrow, tall, and quiet, and the eyes of tribe justice never saw him.

"Go," said Aemil's father, leader of all; they went.

Following his quarry wasn't straightforward—the other boy knew how to vanish in the trees, and the rules said to go his own way. Jense ducked the tribe's expectant gaze. He ran without sound into the tangle of green and grey and black that absorbed him and blocked out all other worlds.

At noon he followed a trail of broken stems and paralyzed bodies to Quicevit, and found him holding the familiar blowgun. A crash of snapped branches marked someone's fall three yards distant. Jense's hands shook, his gun shook.

Quicevit turned. The first dart skimmed past and was lost.

Four more—and how many left in Quicevit's supply? Jense threw himself into the trees, sucking in breath and darting for openings that would force the tall boy to duck. Something light struck his vest. He fumbled back and grabbed the dart half-lodged there—a cold sliver he couldn't read in haste, the barbs lost in leather; he threw it down.

Speed was Jense's advantage. He gained distance. At last he dared to scramble up into a stunted, dying tree, and waited.

Quicevit approached the clear space that this perch bordered slowly, warily, and by this Jense knew he recognized it. Deep blue flowers sprawled just beyond the reach of afternoon sunlight. Jense's aunt planted them, after.

The second dart struck its target.

The other boy rocked back as the curse took hold. He was petrified for a different reason than his victims; he no longer saw the world, and when sound came it was horrible. He bellowed and gasped for air he couldn't keep. The sobs were torn out of him by what grief Jense well knew. And he moved, yes—he fell to the ground, hands splaying out to catch him too late. He landed on a flower and crushed it.

Quicevit fumbled at his belt then, and Jense dropped and ran as he realized the purpose. He grabbed Quicevit's arm and sought the knife. An elbow cracked his rib; pain shocked through him, but panic and rage were a match for despair. He hauled back, seeking better leverage.

How many times was he cut? How many times did he bite and draw blood? He couldn't get the knife away—he couldn't fight forever—

When the shouts distracted him Quicevit took advantage and shoved the knife into his own chest, ending his guilt. His death freed Jense to scream in his stead.

Hard hands dragged him away, cuffed him, silenced him; turned Quicevit over, too late. The magi in her snakeskin clothes wavered in Jense's sight. She took the dart from Quicevit's neck. Someone gripped his arm, the hold like iron. "Take the rest from him," she said once she'd studied it. "They'll burn."

"What—?" asked his captor as other hands moved to do her will.

"A mirror curse. All *he* feels, reflected—" The magi broke off and looked to the corpse. "And yet I do not think the boy died of grief." There were mutters, all ignored, as she crossed the grass: she said to him,

"Show me where."

He had to pull away from the hold to expose the tissue on his shoulder, white and pink with black at its heart where he'd failed to cut the barb free. She placed her fingers on him and whispered words that made Jense scream anew—but then it was in her hand. One look; the magi made a fist and crushed it. "Your curse was brutal, terrible, far crueler than a game allows."

"It was justice!" His voice had grown rust.

She nodded. "As I said."

While he struggled with that she spoke to the man at his side. "How many others?"

"Two." It was Aemil's father. "Loicha's curses broke three boys' bones and Mandan crippled Illes; she won't recover."

The agate chains were hooked to the magi's belt, and she counted out three. "You'll be a striker," she answered Jense's stare. "You will—in Quicevit's place."

They drew him away, to the feast and the honor he'd never recognized as a mark of cruelty.

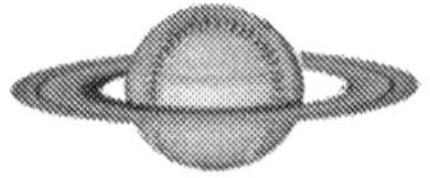

Amanda M. Hayes was born in Indianapolis and received her BA in English from Indiana University in 2002. She's since lived in Oklahoma, Missouri, and Virginia, each of which has been inspiring in its own way. Her first sale came on her eighteenth birthday; between then and now she has seen her fiction in such publications as *Shadow Box*,

Farthing, *Allegory*, and *Raven Electrick*.

Librarian Gladiators

Richard Pitaniello

Stomps thundered, rattled the bleachers and *boomed* through the gym, shaking lights on the high ceiling. Fists swirled in the air, hands cupped over mouths. The crowd chanted: "Hec-a-te! Hec-a-te! Hecate Hecate heck heck heck!" Cheerleaders thrashed and sang: "Can't be beat! Can't be beat! Rockin' rockin' Hecate!"

The librarian witch in the black-rubber trench coat and sharp, black hat ignored the crowd. *Must focus*, she reminded herself. *Focus and kill.*

She stared at her two remaining opponents: Circe, wielding an endless supply of razor-edged cards and a military strength barcode laser; and Warlock, riding a motorcycle and swinging one of those heavy bathroom keychains as large as a steak.

Amateurs, Hecate sneered. *Time to die.*

Circe threw a razor card. Hecate spit toxin, striking it in mid-flight, dissolving it and eating a hole through the floor. Circe fired her laser and burned a pit into Hecate's chest, spewing a cloud of acrid smoke. Hecate gasped, laughed, hissed: "Sssssshhh!"

Warlock revved his motorcycle and charged. Hecate jumped over him, flipped, landed cat-like. Circe threw two cards. Hecate dived, but one twisted and cut her, spraying green blood from her arm. Hecate *Sssshhhed* again.

Circe fired, scorching craters in floorboards and bricks. Then she fired at the supports of the gym's basketball backboard. It snapped loose and plummeted, shattering against the floor, catching Hecate's arm.

The crowd gasped.

Hecate pushed the backboard away with her magic and stood up, one arm limp. She raised her good hand, yelled incantations.

Then the gym ceiling stretched and swirled like clouds, forming a tornado of distorted plaster and metal. A hole in the bottom sucked and slurped. Circe frantically threw cards at Hecate...but the funnel swallowed Circe and retracted. The ceiling returned to normal but every light in the gym smoldered red, casting black shadows.

The crowd cheered and stomped. Cheerleaders thrashed.

Warlock swung his enormous bathroom keychain and took a run at Hecate with the motorcycle. He threw the keychain, striking her hard in the chest.

"Can't outrun motorcycles, lady!" Warlock sneered.

Hecate wheezed: "Can't outrun lightning, Warlock!"

Tires squealed. The motorcycle raced forward.

Hecate shrieked an incantation and white-blue fire shot out her fingertips, lighting the entire gym and blasting Warlock into black ash and bone. The gym faded back to red. The crowd stood and applauded. An announcer stepped out. "Well, dang it everybody! That was the best episode of Librarian Gladiators yet! Such suspense! Such terror! Such artistry!"

The crowded howled. "I know, I know," the announcer assured them. "Now let's have one last round of applause!"

The gym reverberated with noise. Hecate raised her good arm above her head and limped into the locker room, where doctors waited for her under nice, white lights. She sat down on the bench, glanced out the window.

On the other side of the window, librarians picketed the gym, chanting: "The end of slander is long overdue!" "Ssssh happens, but we do more!" "Reference folks referee, not reprimand!"

"Crybabies," Hecate muttered, shaking her head.

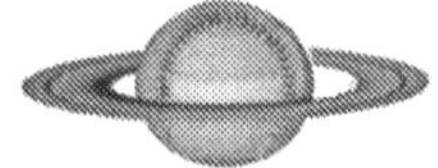

Richard Pitaniello lurks in backwoods forests, Latin halls, and librarian grad-school. He enjoys typing spreadsheet inventories of his own monstrously-swollen library, and it irks him that he cannot arrange his books alphabetically and by size at the same time. His writing is mostly a horror quagmire, though he does venture into other genres. He has been published in *Dreams and Nightmares*, *Florida Horror* (Carnifex Press), *Black Petals*, *Wicked Karnival*, and *Mount Zion*. "Librarian Gladiators" was loosely inspired by his high school experience. Rick seldom partakes in sports himself.

Mutiny

Erin Kinch

The colonel's hat sat askew on his tiny, blue head and he was missing a plastic boot, but his stern expression did not waver. "I have never lost in battle. Surrender is preferable to slaughter."

"I'm in charge!" Jess glared at her ragtag troops. "*Attack*!"

None of them—not the army soldiers, cavalry, revolutionaries, or red coats—moved to obey. Not even the young revolutionary in the corner hiding his eyes under his tri-cornered hat—Pee-Wee's hesitation hurt Jess most of all.

Across the hexagonal board, Lexie giggled. Her recently purchased army, led by a barbarian princess clad in fur and leather, stood in a loose chevron, still in pristine condition. Over the course of the game, they'd claimed three-fourths of the board. If the colonel surrendered, they won just as if they had captured him.

"I told you fantasy troops were the best." Lexie's smug tone made Jess want to smack her supposed best friend. Lexie's allowance was twice as big, so she didn't have to deal with an army mostly cobbled together from her brother's hand-me-down troops. While Jess spent the game keeping order among dissenting factions, Lexie sat back and let her troops do all the work.

Jess assessed her battalion one last time. Their line had broken under the last assault, and now the soldiers stood in scattered clumps of three and four. A third of their original number had vanished into Lexie's P.O.W. cell.

Only three of Lexie's first wave occupied Jess's cell—the centaur cavalry had trampled the bulk of her infantry. Before disappearing into P.O.W. status, the colonel's second-in-command had been crushed by flailing hooves, sending a plastic arm and leg flying over the edge of the board.

The colonel straightened his hat and crossed his arms over his chest, obscuring a row of medals. "That horde controls the battle field, and we don't have the position for an attack. Surrender is the only choice."

Jess leaned closer, allowing her black curls to fall forward, shielding her whispers from Lexie's all-too-interested ears. "We have to attack kamikaze-style—plan beta-9. If Pee-Wee can capture the princess, victory is ours."

The colonel glared at Pee-Wee. The only fighters shorter than him were Lexie's axe-wielding dwarves. Pee-Wee was Jess's first real contribution to the battalion, and the colonel was not pleased. Pee-We had yet to see action.

"Beta-9 is suicide. General Roger never…"

"Forget Roger!" Jess snapped, oblivious of Lexie. "Roger traded you to me. I'm general now, and I'll court-martial anyone who doesn't follow my orders." The colonel flinched, and Jess pressed her advantage. "It's me or the garbage chute, Colonel."

The colonel's glare didn't soften, but he inclined his head in acceptance, then yelled, "Atten-hut!" The troops jerked to attention, despite torn uniforms and missing accessories. Then the colonel called, "Attack on the general's mark!"

Jess glanced at Pee-Wee. He'd been so bold at the toy store, full of innovative strategy. Would he come through, or had his purchase been a blunder? Pee-Wee winked.

"This is taking forever," Lexie complained. "*Manic Playhouse* is on soon. I don't want to miss the song of the day."

"Troops," Jess commanded, "proceed with attack plan beta-9."

Hooves thundered across the board's green and brown hexagons as her beleaguered cavalry charged the remaining centaurs. A horse screamed as a centaur lance pierced its heart. Lexie shrieked as another centaur was hit with a musket ball and vanished.

On the other side of the chevron, foot soldiers descended on the archers with a vengeance, shouting the names of their fallen comrades as a battle cry. A lanky soldier vanished as an arrow pierced his shoulder, followed by three more in rapid succession. But the infantry pressed on through the barrage of arrows, despite heavy casualties, until they were close enough to engage the archers in hand-to-hand combat. Helpless in close quarters, archers began to disappear, as well.

The chevron disintegrated as soldiers fought to stay in the game. First one side took a victory, then the other. Jess urged her troops on, directing the flow. Lexie's well-heeled troops looked to their warrior queen for orders.

"Kill them all!" Lexie cried uselessly. The princess shouted orders, but without a cohesive battle strategy Lexie's army began to falter. Pee-Wee crept forward, slipping from one hexagon to the next without engaging in a fight. No one on the opposing side noticed the tiny revolutionary. He circumnavigated the infantry-archer skirmish, ducked behind a centaur's hindquarters, and then, when the princess turned the other way, he sprinted over the last hexagon and pressed his musket to the back of her head.

Everyone froze. The dwarves and a centaur lunged for their leader, but Pee-Wee fired first. The musket's report echoed through the living room, and the princess vanished. The rest of Lexie's forces knelt to Jess, who sprang from her chair and danced with glee.

"Whatever." Lexie stalked toward the door. "This is a stupid game. I'm going to watch TV."

Jess opened her leather carrying case, and her soldiers marched in single file reverting to their frozen state as they left the game board's animation field. Pee-Wee whooped upon approach and gave Jess a high five, slapping his hand against her extended pinkie. When Jess released her prisoners, Lexie's cell opened as well, and the troops sorted themselves out.

The colonel paused by the princess and kissed her hand. "You almost won, m'dear."

The princess blushed beneath her flesh-colored paint. "You have a good general."

The colonel glanced at Jess. "She acquitted herself adequately for her first foray into the field."

Jess gestured to the carrying case, and the colonel nodded farewell to the princess. "Creativity runs in your family, General." The colonel saluted and then stepped into his slot, freezing into inanimate plastic as the case clicked shut.

Erin Kinch has been writing all her life. She's tried journalism, blogging, and technical writing, as well as many styles in between, but genre fiction is her passion. In 2005, Erin earned a Master's degree in English with an emphasis in creative writing from the University of North Texas. Now she lives and writes in Fort Worth, Texas. Though she has yet to see it with her own eyes, Erin knows beyond a shadow of a doubt that her toys come to life when she leaves the room.

Dealing in Tarot

Ruth Berman

At Witchery U. in the student union
Tarot decks are used for bridge.
Prophecy profs complain,
But kids don't always want to know
Just what it bodes
In health, in heart, in grade-point-averages,
When they don't get long, strong suits.
They just want to forget awhile.

"Shut up and deal," they say,
And don't pull out their handbooks to find out
The meaning of hands that always lose
The Queen-Knave finesse.

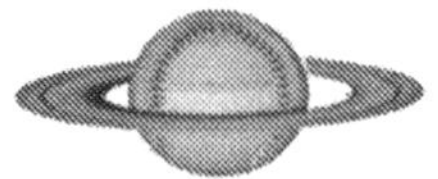

Ruth Berman's work has appeared in many science fiction, general, and literary magazines and anthologies, including *Asimov's*, *Tales of the Unanticipated, Fantasy & Science Fiction*, *Jewish Currents*, and *Cats Magazine.* She has two volumes of translations forthcoming from

Wildside of fiction by 19th century French fantasist Charles Nodier. Berman has edited *Dear Poppa* (Minnesota Historical Society), *The Kerlan Awards in Children's Literature* (Pogo Press), and *Sissajig and Other Surprises* (International Wizard of Oz Club).

The Court Photographer

Lawrence Schimel

Kristy McGovern was a freelance photographer for *The Boston Globe* with an assignment to cover a home game between the Celtics and the Lakers. For a game on both Halloween and a Wednesday night, Kristy wondered how big the turnout would be. She flashed her Media Pass at the ticket collector and made her way up to the media seats. Most of them were already taken—the media working both Wednesdays and Halloween—but she managed to find an empty seat next to a photographer for *The Harvard Crimson.* She smiled at him, but knew they'd be competing as fiercely as the players for the best photos.

As they waited for the game to begin Kristy checked her equipment. While wiping the lens she saw a flash of color out of the corner that made her look up: walking down one of the stands was a tall man who seemed to be shining a bright fuchsia. Kristy brought her camera up and took a few shots of him. *Wow! What a great costume!* she thought. He saw her taking his picture and struck various poses. Around her, the other photographers raced to their cameras, but then waited, poised but unsure what they were supposed to be shooting. *Don't they see him?* Kristy wondered to herself. She couldn't see how they could miss him, he was glowing so brightly. Looking back to reassure herself, she found him gone as well. She scanned the crowd for his purple glow towering over them, but could not find him anywhere. At least she had gotten him on film.

"What was that?" *The Crimson* photographer asked her, when she lowered her camera. "A false alarm or practice shooting?"

"Just starting my roll with some interesting crowd shots."

From down the row, Kristy could here the angry mutters of "Waste of film." But she was sure she had seen him. Again she saw a flash of color out of the corner of her eye, a bright kelly green. When she turned to locate its source she found herself staring at a young woman who stood near the edge of the court striking various poses and shining as brightly as a Japanese Beetle sunning itself on a rose. None of the other photographers seemed to notice her. Nor, for that matter, did the fans. But no matter how many times Kristy looked away and then back she was still there posing for her. So Kristy took a shot of her. In the space between seeing the girl through the lens and looking for her over the top of the camera she was gone.

"Is this your first game or something?" *The Crimson* photographer asked her. "You should save the film for the game."

Kristy flushed at his rebuke and immediately saw a woman glowing red and swirling across the court towards her. She moved like liquid fire over the court and seemed to etch new boundaries for the game in a light trail behind her. A ways off, seeming to dance with her, or at least to the same pattern, was her partner, glowing the same vivid red. As they passed each other near the center Kristy took their picture, quickly looking to her left when she was done.

"I give up," *The Crimson* photographer said.

True to his word, he looked at her sharply a few times when she took more shots of them, glowing brightly and posing for her, but refrained from commenting further on what he thought were simply random shots. But Kristy did see them, she was sure of that. It was not, however, until the start of the game that she realized who they were.

They converged on the Celtics' side of the court, making it a riot of colors, like a large box of crayons strewn across the floor when drawings were abandoned in favor of a trip to the park. But it was the creatures who gathered with the Lakers on the other side of the court who tipped Kristy off to their identity. Opposing the glowing people were the various members of the Unseelie court, goblins and trolls, disheveled giants and assorted other dark beasties of the night. Nan was probably spinning like a steamroller in her grave with shame that Kristy hadn't recognized the Seelie court at first sight after all the stories Nan had told her about them. But Kristy had never expected to see them, let alone in Boston, even on a Samhain eve.

As the mortal teams gathered as well, both courts looked prepared to go to war. *If these pictures only come out right...* No, she couldn't finish for fear she might ruin them herself with a careless thought. She rapped against the wooden underside of her seat. Superstitions seemed quite viable in light of what she was seeing now.

And then the whistle blew and the ball was in motion; there was no more time for idle thoughts. The Celtics had the ball and were heading down the court until a steel-colored troll knocked the ball from a player's hands. The crowd drew a collective breath to see a fumble so early. But the hiss of their second sharp intake followed so closely on the first, when an orange Seelie woman bounced the ball back to the original

Celtic, that they were nearly full to bursting with indrawn breath. Not trusting himself to dribble, despite his miraculous recovery, he took a wild shot from too far away and it landed on the edge. But while everyone expected it to bounce away it dropped neatly into the basket as the tall purple man tapped it in. The game was off to an unbelievably lucky start.

By halftime, the crowd, the referees, and players, all were dumfounded by the string of coincidences that had put the Celtics ahead by 82 points thanks to the aid of the Seelie court. They had expertly blocked the Unseelie fouls, and added their own little stitcheries to tip the balance in their favor. Getting hold of the ball for a few seconds as it lay still after one of the baskets, a Hob had managed to sew some charms into the ball itself. Most spectacular, of course, had been the glowing red couple, executing perfect arabesques and lifting a bewildered Celtic so high as he jumped for a dunk shot that he nearly missed the basket, unused to shooting from so high above the net.

Kristy had gotten great shots of the leap, as she had seen it coming and guessed it before the other photographers had even realized it had happened. *The Crimson* photographer began to reconsider his earlier judgements of her somewhat erratic shootings. She seemed to be able to foretell the great photo opportunities, as if she was watching the game from five minutes ahead. He began training his camera on the spaces she did, although he still lagged behind by a margin of seconds that proved to be the crucial fraction in getting the perfect shots. Kristy noticed his mimicking of her movements and although amused, decided to take some pictures of the Seelie members who sat on the sidelines to throw him off her trail. But he persisted, and she contented herself with being the one to call the shots.

When the battle was over between the Seelie and Unseelie courts, Kristy was not surprised by the carnage; the Celtics slaughtered the Lakers by over 150 points, winning 174 to the Lakers' 12. It was a game, the likes of which had never been seen, and undoubtedly would never be seen again, unless some Samhain eve an Irish team was playing when the Seelie courts were held. But Kristy had gotten photographs of it all, and they'd even posed for her, knowing somehow that she could see them. It was as if she'd been designated court photographer.

But of course, not a single Seelie member showed up on the prints, once Kristy had them drying in her darkroom. She had gotten some wonderful shots, and they ran a series of twelve of them to accompany a four page article on the most incredible game ever seen. It was rivaled by none of the other papers, although a few photos in the spread of *The Harvard Crimson* came close to Kristy's own shots, but were a crucial few seconds out of sync. Still, she was impressed that he had managed to follow her that closely.

The puzzle of the Sidhe, and their photographic disappearance, bothered Kristy for a time. She decided that, since film is developed with silver emulsifiers, the Faerie folk, like werewolves, did not register with it. But Nan's stories had always cited iron as anathema to the Faerie folk, and further research confirmed this, and showed the Sidhe as lovers of jewelry made from silver and gold. And if they weren't going to show up on film, why had they posed so insistently for her? But Kristy let the matter drop from her mind as she resolved to simply ask them, next

Samhain eve.

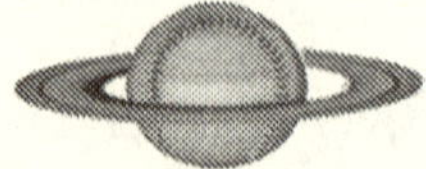

Lawrence Schimel (New York, 1971) is a full-time author, anthologist, and translator whose books include *Fairy Tales for Writers*, *Two Boys in Love*, *The Drag Queen of Elfland*, *Tarot Fantastic*, *La aventura de Cecilia y el dragón*, *Little Pirate Goes to School*, etc. He won the Rhysling Award in 2002 for his poem "How to Make a Human." His writings have been translated into many languages, including Basque, Croatian, Dutch, Esperanto, Finnish, French, German, Greek, Hungarian, Indonesian, Italian, Japanese, Polish, Russian, and Spanish. He lives in Madrid, Spain.

Games People Play

Michael Ceraolo

It started way back in the 1990s
when a chess computer first conquered Kasparov,
                                                                                                    and
continued step-by-step from then on;
                                                                              first,
with the race-walking robots of the early twenty-first century
and on down through dozens of decades
and the whole spectrum of sports,
                                                                         until
only one still remained being played by humans:
basketball
There were attempts at building basketball 'bots,
                                                                                                   but
these were always defeated by the humans
they tried in vain to replace
                                                               And
such human dominion would continue
for as long as the human players could create moves,
                                                                                                        or
even subtle variations on existing moves,
would continue until the death of imagination

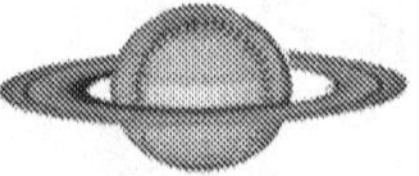

Michael Ceraolo is a fortysomething civil servant/poet trying to overcome a middle-class upbringing. He is the author of two poetry collections *Euclid Creek* (Deep Cleveland Press) and *Cleveland Haiku* (Green Panda Press).

"Games People Play" first appeared in *KillPoet*, Volume 1, Issue 1.

The Drop Zone

Alison J. Littlewood

It was the clearest, most beautiful sky, and the clouds were child's-drawing perfect. I could see it through the plane window, over Aidan's head. I kept trying to catch his eye, but he resolutely stared at the floor between his knees. He was to jump first. Then it was my turn, just like last time.

My nerves had kicked in when I saw him on the ground, his distinctive blue suit standing out from the others, and I wondered why I hadn't heard of this competition. I hadn't entered. The joining papers were delivered, fully paid up, and I knew even then it was a challenge. Aidan wanted another chance to win.

He always wore sky blue, and it always made me crazy. He became one with the air, making his balletics a waste; no one could see them, and it took too long. Who the hell flew in the colour of the sky? Why spend so long in freefall that the next jumper ends up on top of you? It was his own fault, I told myself, but deep down, I knew it was not.

I had cut in on him at the last moment, forcing him to swerve, giving him no chance to turn again. It was an accuracy competition, and nearest to the drop zone won. Aidan hadn't placed. I took first. A spur of the moment thing, an opportunity taken: I wasn't proud of it.

The buzzer sounded and Aidan crouched in the hatch. "See you in the drop zone, buddy," he shouted over the high burr of the plane, his tone friendly, but with a strange look in his eyes. He flipped backwards and was gone, outwards and down.

After the required interval I cleared the plane, turned head first, and plummeted towards the ground. It spread out, clear green like a child's play mat, but I wasn't here for the view. I was looking for the zone.

Then he was there. Straight below me, a flash of light on the arc of his body, turning slow somersaults in the air. I flipped myself back, too quickly. The updraft threw me upwards, spinning but ungainly, not like him. I steadied myself, arms out, and settled into a braced position. He wasn't far off. It was like he was standing in the sky, his arms crossed, staring up at me.

And then I realised how he loved this, the flight, the freedom. He belonged, as though his element was the air, not the earth; he hung there as though gravity wouldn't hold him. When I drew level he turned in a slow circle, holding out his arms, inviting me in. I acknowledged him with a wave, non-committal. He came closer, circling, still staring at me. His eyes were blue like his suit, pale chips of sky embedded in a pale face, and they seemed to get larger, like he was sucking me in. He kept staring. The sky started to grow dark, a storm coming maybe, but all I could see were those chips of light...

Beep.

I was turning in it, drowning in it, air and peace...

Beep.

And the *quiet*, the unbelievable *silence*...

Beep. Beep.

Christ. The sound registered, a warning note from my audible. Not the first emergency tone or the second but the third, the final altitude warning. I pulled the ripcord then glanced at its screen, CANOPY MODE flashing, the drag of the chute finally taking hold. A brief second of looking down, everything dark, and then crashing; for a moment it felt solid, I bent my knees, feared breaking my legs, but then something gave and realised I wasn't over land, at all.

I plunged straight down into it, the cold dark closing over my head.

I swam upward through water that felt slimy, almost viscous. Breaking the surface, I flung off strings of weed that clung to my arms. The water was all around. It was deepest blue-green-grey, like oil. Across the surface, it seemed for miles, there was a coating of the same black weed. I couldn't see into it. I couldn't see the shore.

All I could think was, this wasn't on the map. It shouldn't be here. I shook my head, trying to clear my vision. It shouldn't be anywhere.

I unclipped the chute and spread my arms to float more easily, afraid of being dragged under. The water was buoyant, like a living thing. But cold. The sky was a deep metal grey, clouded over maybe. I couldn't see the sun, not even a glint of where it should be. All around, there was nothing.

They had to send a boat. They had to. They must realise what had happened, when I didn't make it...

Except that this place hadn't been on the map.

I tried to peer into the depths, dreading what might be down there.

Fighting panic, I tried to focus on what I could do. I had no whistle, not in my competition gear. No phone. No light, only the dim backlight on my altimeter. But it was a long time 'til nightfall; surely they would pick me up by then. Someone would come. I listened for the drone of a boat, the hum of a plane. There was no sound. I started to shiver.

Damn Aidan. Where the hell was this? I remembered those eyes of his, pale like pieces of the sky, like light. Like his element. It reminded me of flying up there, him at home in the air, me heavier, not so elegant, not a part of it. Taking a chance when it came, devious, slippery...like water, maybe. But most of all, I thought of his eyes.

And I remembered my own reflected in a mirror after the last jump, leaning my head against the glass. The regret. The way it made them darker, a heavy shade, a deep blue-grey-green, like guilt. Like pain. Like deep, deep water.

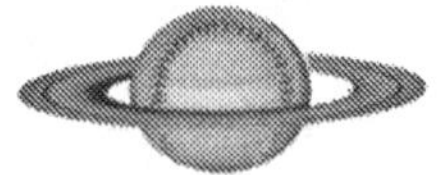

Alison J. Littlewood lives with partner Fergus in West Yorkshire, England, where she spends far too much time dreaming and writing strange notes to herself on scraps of paper. She has contributed to *Whispers of Wickedness*, *Scifantastic*, *Static Movement*, *The Harrow*, *Alien Skin* and the *Thou Shalt Not...* anthology from Dark Cloud Press. As well as a writer of dark tales, she is a slush reader and reviewer for *Whispers of*

Wickedness magazine. See her website at http://alisonlittlewood.co.uk.

Leiris of Green Wyvern United

K.M. Praschak

Two female champions before me
stood on this trampled field,
staring at the cloud-streaked sky
while children shrieked for their heads.

Two decades past, Galenah stole the ball
for more than a dozen aerial carries;
afterwards, she slid into the pits,
her belly torn by the foes' claws.

Three years ago, Arrem of Undertown
accepted the poison-tipped spears
of her cocksure male opponents,
then claimed the win by a single point.

Today, I sniffed the doubt staining
my teammates' armor. Despite this,
I'll capture that scrawny king's cup
and salute all of our momentary victories.

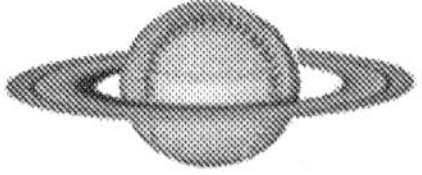

K.M. Praschak's poems have appeared in *Raven Electrick* and *Star*Line.* Her novella "Paragon" is available in *The Amityville House of Pancakes 3* (Creative Guy Publishing). When she isn't swinging a wooden sword or a keyboard around, she likes to play *Final Fantasy XII* and the collectible card game *Magic: The Gathering.*

Ping-Pong Ambition

Larry Hodges

Toby, one-half inch tall, screamed and banged his fists on the rounded white walls of his prison. From outside he could hear the fading hysterical laughter of the genie who had imprisoned him in the ping-pong ball. How could this have happened?

All he had wanted was to be the greatest ping-pong player ever. Instead, he was stuck in this ball, just himself and the thick, red book the genie had given him. He let loose another set of screams.

When he finally calmed down, he sat cross-legged on the celluloid floor and sobbed quietly to himself for a time. Then he opened the book, *Magic of the Djinni.* It was four inches thick, with seemingly normal paper, and yet, paging to the back, he saw that it contained ten million pages. He began to read, starting in the A's.

He read about Abominable Snowmen, the making of, and decided to try the spell. He created one, right there in the ping-pong ball. The creature roughed him up, but fortunately it tired before killing him, and he was able to read ahead and learn about Amulets for protection.

Then he was on to learning about Adepts, the Alexandrian Path of Witchcraft, Antipathetic Magic, and much more.

The first few hundred years were tedious. Often he'd throw down the book and attack the walls with every spell he'd learned so far. But nothing could break through, not even Astrology or Aztec Magic. His powers ended at the walls of the ping-pong ball.

Finally, after four hundred years, he reached the B's, and learned how to handle Boredom. As he continued to develop his powers, life became more comfortable. He furnished his prison with all the comforts of home.

As the eons went by his skin became wrinkled and gray, and his dark hair turned white and fell out. He decided his age was a badge of honor, and so did not use the Beautification spells he had learned. He still felt young on the inside.

When he reached the P's, he learned all the magic needed for ping-pong. He created his own ping-pong table, net, rackets and balls. By folding the far side of the ping-pong table to vertical, he could play against the rebounds and rally by himself, just as he used to do before his imprisonment. He spent many a happy afternoon practicing over the next few thousand years.

At the rate of one thousand pages per year, a little less than three pages per day, he slowly worked his way through all the magic in the book. Finally, after ten thousand years, he put the book down for the last time, having mastered the intricacies of zombies. He now had all the powers of a genie. And yet he was still a prisoner.

Then he heard a sound from outside. He put his ear against the walls, and there was no question about it. It was the sound of ping-pong. Suddenly his world turned upside down, throwing him off his feet. His lounge chair and ping-pong table barely missed crashing into him. Something smashed into the side of his ping-pong prison, slamming him against the wall. His world spun about.

Again something smashed into his prison, and again he and the ball's contents slammed against the wall. It happened over and over and over. Whoever was playing ping-pong outside was using Toby's prison as the ball.

There was a sudden screeching sound. His ball had cracked! It was only a slit, but that was all he needed. Grasping the book, he turned himself into smoke and escaped through the thin gap. Outside he solidified himself at full size. Finally, after ten thousand years, he was *free*!

A man holding a ping-pong paddle was staring at him. Toby stared back, and then fought back laughter. Could it be? The man had been playing ping-pong by himself, with one side of the table folded to vertical, just as Toby had done for so many years. *He still has his hair*, Toby thought, feeling about where he had once had that hair.

"I have been trapped in that ping-pong ball for ten thousand years," Toby said. "For freeing me by cracking that ball, I grant you one wish."

The man was hyper-ventilating, a reasonable reaction when a genie suddenly appears out of a ping-pong ball. Finally he caught his breath.

"Well," said the man, "what I really want is to be the greatest ping-pong player ever."

Yes, Toby thought, *and boy are you going to regret not wishing for that!*

"But that would be a waste," the man continued. "I can wish for anything, right?"

"Anything in my power," Toby said, "and just about anything *is* in my power."

"Then," the man said, a huge grin on his face, "I wish to have all the powers of a genie. Then I can wish to be the greatest ping-pong player ever, and still have *more* wishes!"

Toby couldn't hold it back any longer, and began to laugh. The thousands of years of frustration now came out in relieved giggles, hoots, snickers and guffaws as the man looked at him in surprise.

"You *will* have the powers of a genie," Toby finally said between giggles. He handed the book to the man. "It'll take you ten thousand years to learn, so study well!" He pointed a finger at his younger self, turning him to smoke, and with a gesture moved him into the cracked ping-pong ball.

Laughing hysterically, he sealed the crack, put an impervious spell on the walls, and transported it ten thousand years into the past so that it would reappear here at the end of that time. Then he eyed the ping-pong table, and his laughter turned to pure joy. With thousands of years of practice, he wouldn't even need to use magic to be the greatest ping-pong player ever.

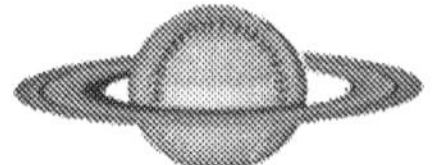

"Science fiction & fantasy, and table tennis—that's my life!" says **Larry Hodges** of Germantown, MD. He's an active member of the Science Fiction & Fantasy Writers of America, with 14 short story sales, and is a graduate of the 2006 Odyssey Fantasy Writer's Workshop. He also has a Master's in journalism to go with a Bachelor's degree in math. Larry is a member of the USA Table Tennis Hall of Fame with a long career in the Olympic sport as a player, coach, editor and writer, and has two books and over 1000 articles (in 65 different publications) on table tennis. Visit him at http://www.larryhodges.org.

Virtual Pong Circa 35,000 B.C.

G. O. Clark

All that's needed
is a sunny day, tired eyes,
and a little peace
and quiet.

To play, simply
shut your eyes, turn your
back to the sun, and
concentrate.

The object of the
game is to keep a dust mote
in motion until it dissolves,
or consciousness wanes.

With a little
patience, the solitary
player can keep this effect alive
for a considerable time.

Some players say

the dust motes remind them of
other things, like snakes,
birds, or bones,

but purists of the
game tend to agree, players of
this ilk would be better off just
staring at the clouds.

Only one player can win.
One player lose. As it were,
one in the same, which is the only
rule of the game.

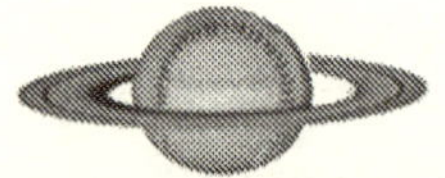

G. O. Clark lives and works in Davis, CA, where soccer moms vie for SUV parking spaces, and the college marching band is well medicated. His latest book of poems is *25 Cent Rocket Ship to the Moon* from Dark Regions Press (2007). For more career stats, see his webpage at http://hometown.aol.com/goclarkpoetry/clark.html.

"Virtual Pong Circa 35,000 B.C." first appeared in *Pirate Writings*, Vol. 4, No. 4, 1996.

Night Vaulting

Camille Alexa

In my dreams, I flew.

I'd never pole-vaulted in waking life. But for the past thirty-two months, three weeks and two days, in dreams I vaulted over pit and crowd and sky at the end of a pole. At night, the slender stalk of aluminum and fiberglass in my chalky grip planted itself—an extension of my spine and lungs and the muscles of my arms—in the ground and shot me through the air, and I flew. Beneath, the garish motley of spectators in over-bright tee-shirts undulated. All sound ceased except the pumping of my heart. The zenith moment was not brief, but elastic, sustained. My body hung suspended, in absolute success and physical perfectitude, without weight.

And then I would twist and fall. When my back slammed into the mat I would wake, gasping with the impact; crying, struggling upright, sucking breaths between sobs.

John would quiet my flailings, my beating heart, my despair. Often, neither of us could return to sleep. He'd lift me into my chair and wheel me to the kitchen. He'd make coffee, and dawn would creep across the sky, apologetic.

When John assured himself I was fine, he would wheel my chair into the den, where I spent mornings reading while he took his own wheels—the beautiful Italian bicycle he loved as much as he loved me—and they would ride the fresh morning trails together amid the dewdrops and the opening petals of wildflowers. That was their romance: dew and flowers and unfettered sunshine.

At dinner John served salad, then poured me another glass of wine.

His bicycle leaned against the dining room wall. He claimed it was easier to wheel it here, through the sliding-glass patio doors, than take it all the way around to the garage. Sometimes he forgot to put it away, and at night, when I wasn't sailing through the sky at the end of a pole, I could hear the bicycle all the way from my bedroom.

"You all right, Catherine?" asked John. "The anniversary's coming up, but it's been nearly three years. I'd hoped...."

"Thirty-two months, three weeks and three days," I said.

He reached across the table and placed his hand over mine. "It was nobody's fault," he said. "Just an accident. A stupid, horrible accident."

I looked at the rumpled napkin in my lap, corners sticking out like the wings of broken doves. "I didn't mention fault," I said.

John hadn't driven in thirty-two months, three weeks and three days. Nothing, since the crash, but the bicycle. I turned my head to watch it lean against the wall. My chair looked stocky and reliable next to the Italian's streamlined curves.

After dinner, John wheeled me to bed. He helped me undress and laid the sheets across my body; across the thick dead logs of my legs. He and the Italian went for an evening ride; "Just a turn about the field," he said.

They left by the dining room patio door. Even from the bedroom, I heard the click of the latch. My chair sat by the window, motionless, staring in the direction of my departing husband and his wheels.

That night I woke gasping for breath into darkness, clutching my breast with the hand which moments before had gripped the slender tower of fiberglass and vaulted me high above the bar like a rocket, like a shot, like a meteorite.

My breathing calmed. The beats of my heart resumed their ordinary rhythm. The scent of freedom and success faded from my nostrils and I lay quiet.

I saw the outline of John's body in the dark. He faced away, his breathing unhurried. The window, where my chair usually waited, was vacant.

I closed my eyes and listened. I could hear my chair in the dining room by the sliding patio doors, its rubber wheels pressed against the glass.

Without waking John I rolled myself onto the floor. I'd felt nothing below the waist for nearly thirty-two months, three weeks and four days. If there were going to be bruises, they wouldn't pain me. If bits of floor dragged and scraped my thighs where my nightgown rode up, I might bleed but unless I looked, I wouldn't know.

My palms were tingly and raw by the time I reached the dining room. My shoulders ached. By moonlight filtering in the patio doors I saw the spokes of my wheels and those of the Italian, glinting, side by side.

The last few feet were the hardest. It took me a moment to catch my breath, but the wheels were patient, and silent.

I fumbled open the lock on the sliding door, pressed both palms against the glass, and thrust it as wide as I could. My chair bounced back from the rough motion. The Italian shuddered, but didn't fall.

The screen was light, and easy to slide aside. The wheels trembled on the edge of the threshold, then the Italian shot past and sped to the edge of the yard, where it hesitated. My chair, heavy and safe, waited.

"Go," I said. "It's all right, really."

The chair bumped over the aluminum threshold and rolled across the night-soaked grasses and curled-up leaves of clover to stand beside the Italian. They then wheeled as one, veered away, and I soon lost sight of them in the tall growth of the field behind the house.

Rather than drag myself back to bed, I slept slumped against the wall. This time, when the pole cracked the whip of itself and vaulted me above the crowd, I flew higher than ever.

I spread my arms. My body soared over countryside and the sprinklings of cities. Flattened against invisible currents, I watched anonymous landscape pass below; patchwork cornfields and the mottled greens of forest. On the edge of the horizon near the rising sun I caught the twinkle of spokes, spinning across the earth as I shot, unapologetic, across the sky.

Camille Alexa enjoys a near-perpetual love affair with words. To her amazement and delight, they sometimes seem to love her back. She has short fiction forthcoming in *Black Box* (Brimstone Press) and *Extra-Terrestrial Ruins* (Hadley Rille Books). She is a full member of Broad Universe and writes for *The Green Man Review.*

Liliya's Game

Jennifer Crow

With the ghost at her back, Liliya recalls the way her toes hurt in her thin leather shoes, and the boy's gap-toothed grin. Memories of that day come in flashes: the medals on her grandfather's jacket pressing between her shoulder blades when she leans into him; the sharp tobacco scent of his friends; the wind tugging at her hair bows. And the boy, tow-headed, bare-kneed, who nudges a ball in her direction.

She hangs back until her grandfather prods her; when she glances over her shoulder, he gives a curt nod. The old men make space for them, shuffling backward. A few—those not too broken by the war—take a kick, their legs made clumsy by time and memory. But mostly they talk, a murmur like the sound of thunder beyond the horizon.

While the old men rustle like pigeons as they put on their coats, the boy bows over Liliya's hand. She wipes his touch away on the skirt of her dress, and she swipes at her cheek when her grandfather kisses her, his whiskers scratchy.

Now she touches that cheek. The boy bounces the ball on his knee: once, twice, a third time. Through the thin walls she hears voices, smells food cooking. She wonders if they, too, have ghosts. Then she realizes, of course they do. In Moscow, so soon after the second revolution, all the ghosts have come home.

She edges past him to the table. The notice, clipped from a neighborhood broadsheet, lies before her. When she takes a seat, not looking at the newspaper clipping, she still feels the bounce of the ball through the chair's legs. The rhythm moves the clipping ever closer to the edge of the table.

"Stop it," she says. And again, louder, "Stop. It!" He falters for a moment, but only a moment. Dust motes shudder in the air.

With trembling hands she scoops up the clipping, holding it away from the light. She rolls it in her fingers like a homemade cigarette, pinches the ends, touches her pockets in a search for matches. Maybe if she set the news ablaze, it would be just a dream. Maybe then the boy would go. She feels him at her shoulder like a breath of winter. If she wants, she can reach up and touch the cold space he inhabits.

"I'll go all over the world," the boy in her memory tells her. "I won't stay here always." She remembers thinking he was fearless, and wanting to say something brave in turn.

"My grandfather says . . ." The words come back to her, the ones she said that day, but she can't say the rest out loud. Even now, tongues in Moscow tangle and fall silent. She finds a book of matches, lights one, and lets it burn down to her fingertips before shaking it out. "My grandfather says . . ."

Maybe they took the boy, too. Maybe men came in the darkness that night, and bundled him up, and searched his house for signs of disloyalty and deceit. Maybe forever after his mother and grandmother spoke in whispers, or glanced at each other and looked away again without words. Maybe they kept the ball under his bed, hoping he'd return someday to use it.

She smoothes the paper under trembling hands. On this side an advertisement for a ZIL auto stares up at her. On the other . . .

On the other side, the past waits. Her mother cut this out and sent it with a note: "You should be here."

But Liliya has lived with the ghost long enough. She turns the thin newsprint over, and her grandfather's face stares up at her. The brief note with his picture tells of a funeral long-delayed, a death the state only now admits.

"I won't stay here always." She lights another match, holds it to the corner of the picture, lets it eat the past.

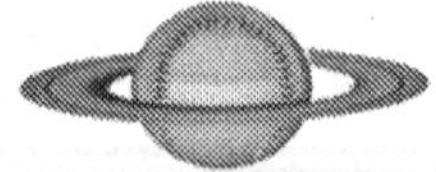

Jennifer Crow began studying Russian in high school, visited what was then the Soviet Union, and quickly fell in love with the history and culture of Russia, so it was only a matter of time before it made an appearance in one of her stories. Jennifer's work has appeared in a number of print and electronic venues, and several of her poems have received honorable mentions in past editions of the *Year's Best Fantasy and Horror*. She lives beside a waterfall near Buffalo, New York.

Gravity Field Golfball

Stephen D. Rogers

Welcome sports fans! There's a full crowd here for today's INTERGALACTIC BOWL and an expected viewership of twenty billion sentient life forms. Wow.

While we wait for the gravity wells to generate and the game to begin, I'd like to share some of the player interviews I conducted earlier today.

First up, Buzz Johnson from the defending champion BLACKHOLES.

"Tell me, Buzz, what goes through your mind as your team racks up an undefeated season?"

"Well, I just try to play one game at a time."

"So you don't approve of player cloning?"

"I can't speak for the team or the league, but I'd hate to have to tackle myself."

Next up, a contemplative moment with Hawk Smith, lowest league scorer two years in a row.

"Hawk, the DYNAMOS were favored in the playoffs until they were knocked out of the running during the last game of the regular season. What happened?"

"We couldn't keep the ball out of our opponent's end zone. I don't really want to go into the formulas right now, but let's just say that our universal gravitational constant was off."

"What does this mean for next year?"

"We'll fire the front office, shuffle our coaches, and raise ticket prices. It's all about the fans."

And finally, Crusher Huntz from the upstart GRAVITRONS.

"Crusher, the GRAVITRONS seemed to come out of nowhere. Did you ever in your wildest dreams imagine that your team would be suiting up this afternoon?"

"Be the ball."

"Excellent advice, Crusher. Crusher? You're floating away."

"Be the ball!"

There you have it, folks. And there's the whistle.

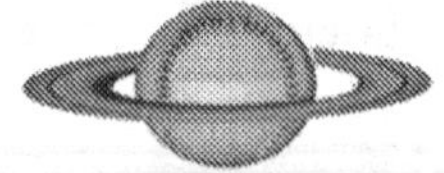

Over four hundred stories and poems by **Stephen D. Rogers** have appeared in more than one hundred publications. His website, http://www.stephendrogers.com, includes a list of new and upcoming titles as well as other timely information. While not a big sports fan by nature, Stephen says his daughter is doing her best to change that.

Space Envelopes

Willow Katsumi Relf-Discartin

Terrie Leigh Relf

there's a field in space
where imaginary lines
are agreed upon
drawn
to separate
one quadrant
from another
one team
from another

between them
a giant box of envelopes
maintains a steady orbit
the scoreboard hovers
just beyond the sidelines where
each team's pulsing colors
pierce through an artificial haze

referees stand by
make note of the cheering crowds

sponsors hold their breaths
waiting to award the victorious
with contracts
transgalactic tours
the usual SWAG

SETI broadcasts
the announcer's diatribe
translated into ten-thousand
different dialects
give or take a few

What could be inside those envelopes?
the viewers murmur
What might each become?

Expect the unexpected...
the announcer intones
a starslip's sail?
a stellar cruiser?
nothing so mundane

viewers lean forward
in self-contained pods
floating chairs—
the domed amphitheatre

at last grows silent as
each team shows off their skills
to arrive at
a universal score

massive bursts of energy ensue
as new planets, exoplanets, and
stellar systems emerge
some with gravity and water
others ringed with methane gas
still others join the panoply

great deals on field-side seats
the ticket scalpers call out
wending through the crowds when
the final envelope is opened. . .
the intricate folds of an origami universe
are revealed and nothing remains of what
once was and what wasn't becomes revealed

SFPA member **Terrie Leigh Relf** is on staff at Sam's Dot Publishing. She also serves as the poetry editor for *Tales from the Moonlit Path*. Her work has appeared in a variety of publications which include

Doorways Magazine, *Scifaikuest*, *Dreams and Nightmares*, *Star*line*, *Tales of the Talisman*, and *The Sword Review*. *Beyond the Workshop*, a collection of her published columns on writing, and *My Friend, the Poet, and Other Poems about People I Think I Know*, a speculative poetry collection, will be available sometime this year or early 2008.

Willow Katsumi Relf-Discartin entered 6th grade this fall. In addition to studying science and playing the cello, she likes to collaborate on poetry and short stories with her mother. Her credits include *The World Haiku Review*, *Beyond Centauri*, *Aoife's Kiss*, *Sol-Magazine*, and others.

Soul in One

Kevin Lightburn

The midnight moon silvered the ninth hole, imbuing it with sinister ambiance. Obsidian felt it the perfect setting for the final destruction of his age-old nemesis.

All the centuries of hunting one another—the chaos and deaths of countless innocents—would end tonight.

His long time familiar, Egan, cowered beside him, golf bag at the ready. Obsidian smiled at the deep bruise on his neck. He had fed on the creature's life energy to bolster him for this challenge.

At that moment, his mortal enemy materialized with a garish puff of smoke.

She was an obese woman, as large as she was arrogant. She had gone by a variety of names throughout the ages, but had settled on one she felt reflected this new millennium—Hilary.

They eyed each other coolly.

"Glad you could come," he said, trying not to cackle with glee. The old bat had fallen for it!

She plucked a mouse from a pouch on her hip and popped it in her mouth. A few terrified squeaks were followed by the wet crunch of bones. "This was your suggestion," she munched as she spoke. "Truly mundane. Only, the stakes were too good to pass up."

It had been an impulsive offer to settle things this way, one he couldn't quite understand himself. Perhaps, despite all her sorcery and tricks, he could finally defeat her in a way in which she could never hope to match him: physical skill.

He had been practicing for centuries. A strange fascination when all was considered. But when you are immortal, hobbies help to pass the time. And he suspected that Hilary had never once picked up a club.

He hefted his. "One hole, one outcome."

Her eyes flickered in the dark. "I win this, and your blighted soul will fuel my spells for an eternity."

He tried not to laugh. "Then let's make this official, shall we?" Together they uttered the oath with words, magical and dark, from a language long dead.

With the oath complete, they both took an involuntary step away from the other. The pact was sealed. Neither could escape nor break it until one was consumed.

"Ladies first," he said. "I would be happy to offer you a club as I see you've forgotten to bring one." *Fool woman.*

"No need," she said, and motioned a hand.

Something staggered drunkenly out from the murk of the tree line. Obsidian frowned. What was this?

The golem was comprised of various mismatched human body parts, sewn together with thick brown thread. Clasped in its grip was a golf club.

He scowled. "This won't be binding—only actual oath-takers can engage in the pact!"

"Ah," Hilary grinned. "Although pieced together from others, the golem is bound with my own hair, and the flesh anointed with my tears. It is an extension of me."

A pang of worry tapped at the back of his mind. Obsidian glared at the golem. This was a reminder of the unholy army of apparitions she once used to attack his castle centuries ago.

The thing shambled awkwardly up to the tee. *How can she expect to win with that?* It could barely stand. *She'd fair better doing it herself, ample girth or not.* Obsidian suppressed a smile.

It paused, then swung, and within that motion, embodied pure elegance. Perfect form, a beautiful swish, and a solid thunk sent the little ball airborne.

Obsidian watched in amazement as he traced its path through the cool night air, then onto the green, where it bounced twice and plopped directly into the hole.

Incredible! Yet, there it was.

Another mouse, more crunching.

He was mortified. But he couldn't stop now, even if he wanted. The pact was active, pulling him along, compelling him to finish what was started. He stepped up to the tee.

He calmed himself, breathed deeply, then hit the ball. He knew, emphatically, that it was the best shot he had ever taken. He would get it —causing a draw and the pact would be negated.

Then he would make his escape from this debacle.

The ball bounced perfectly onto the green, rolled across the trim grass, directly towards the hole. He was going to get it!

Then, bare inches away, something stuck its head up out of the hole.

A mouse.

The ball caromed off its head and rolled away on a new trajectory. The mouse squeaked in fright and darted away.

"Oh, dear," Hilary said. "Imagine that. One of the little rascals must of gotten out." She shook the pouch and smiled.

Obsidian's jaw dropped. He wanted to shriek at her, but couldn't—the pact was already transmuting him, sapping his energies away.

She pointed triumphantly at the golem. "The parts were cultivated from the corpses of golf masters. I've been collecting them for centuries—just for this moment."

"But that's impossible!" His voice crackled, fading by the moment. "I challenged you only weeks ago!"

Egan brushed past him to stand at Hilary's side. She caressed his cheek. "I arranged for you to find Egan, years past, in the hopes he would be one you'd keep. But not before I'd ladened him with a slow-acting spell of suggestion to be cast upon you."

His mind reeled. Could it be? She had planned this all along? Planting the seed that would be his end?

He wanted to scream but could not. His body was transforming, becoming dark, acrid vapor.

Hilary held out a crystal ball which drew him in, to be imprisoned forever.

She smiled and waved. "Thanks for the game."

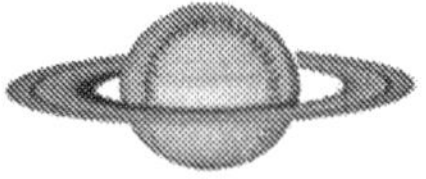

Kevin Lightburn maintains his lair on the western edge of Canada, where graveyards are plentiful, and night security is lax. He enjoys collecting shovels and treadless running shoes.

Menace Anyone

Brian Rosenberger

His first serve
Sudden as a scream
Too fast for the speed gun
Out, yells the line judge
An empty stare follows, already carving
An epitaph in his skull
Heart failure before he's forty
The Reaper, between bounces
Rubs the fuzz with unfeeling fingers
Second serve and the ball floats
For seconds, for eternity
A skeletal stretch
His racquet eclipses the sun
Elegant as a scythe during the harvest
Then...whoosh
Like a long last breath
The ball bounces, rockets at an unnatural angle
Thanks to the topspin
Extra slice always his specialty
His opponent plays tombstone
The ball goes untouched

An Ace

Advantage Death

Now and always

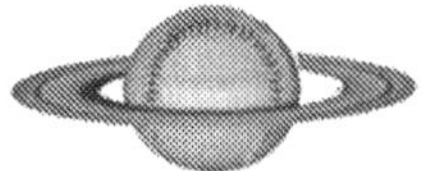

Brian Rosenberger's writing has appeared in *Read By Dawn Vol. 1*, *Cthulhu Sex Magazine*, *Dead Men (and Women) Walking*, *Twisted Cat Tales* and many other publications and personal ads. He has also authored *Pooms that Go SPLAT*. Updates can be found at his website, http://home.earthlink.net/~brosenberger.

Jumping over the Moon

Alex Dally MacFarlane

Hey diddle diddle

The cat and the fiddle

When the stars smallpox the desk with white light and when the alchemist works his metal-magics in another corner of the house, the cat and the fiddle begin to play.

"Tonight's game is jumping over the moon," announces the cat. Its words are punctuated with squeaks from its jaw, not oiled in almost a month. A flick of its wire-tail and the other toys look up at the subject of the cat's gesture: one of the alchemist's desk lamps, its bulb bright and moon-round.

The toys know the game, and hurry to put everything in place. The lamp nudged into place just so, scraps of crumpled paper arranged underneath, the ball—a marble—found.

A minute after the cat's announcement, the fiddle's fingers—bows attached to supple arms of wood—tease a flat melody from its strings, and the game begins.

On stumpy legs of metal, the dish and the spoon chase the marble. The dish picks it up and races towards the lamp, and after three seconds must pass it to the spoon; leaping, legs squeaking, the dog catches it in its mouth and runs towards the cow, whose blue metal skin reflects the bulb's light into the dog's eyes just as it releases the marble, distracting it; the glass ball rolls towards the desk's edge, stopped at the last moment by the cat.

Dog-and-cow or dish-and-spoon? Wild card, playing for either side, the cat pauses and considers.

The game is old, the victors consistent.

The cat passes to the spoon, who bends its head to catch and hold the marble. A flick of its head three seconds later and the dish catches, throws again, but the dog is too nimble and jumps to intercept, hits the marble towards the cow who grips it tight between oversized jaws. The dog crouches and the cow runs, jumps on the dog's back and leaps off, upwards.

The cow jumped over the moon
The little dog laughed to see such sport

Over the moon with the ball and down into the cushion of paper, and the cow joins the dog's laughter. The fiddle plays a triumphant jig while the cat wonders if the crockery will ever win.

The alchemist nudges the fiddle aside with metal-stained fingers, putting a premature end to the music. With a scowl only half of irritation —amusement sneaking in at lip-corners—he tells the toys to "*run off and make a mess elsewhere, I need to work here.*"

"What shall we play next?" says the cow as they hop down the branches of the desk-high moly tree.

The dish and spoon reach the floor first and, looking back up at the others, say in unison, "Something we can win!"

"To the kitchen!" adds the spoon.

And the dish ran away with the spoon

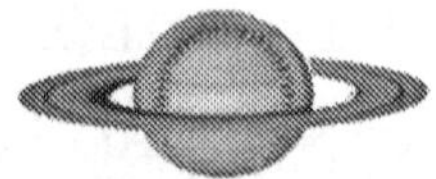

Alex Dally MacFarlane has been writing ever since the discovery of computer games made her think that if stories could be found on a 32-bit cartridge, why not in the mind of an eleven-year-old girl? Now she has a BA in War Studies and History from King's College London and works just outside London, proofreading military specifications. Her short fiction has sold to magazines including *Shimmer*, *Sybil's Garage* and *Farrago's Wainscot*, and her poetry to *Goblin Fruit.* You can find her on Livejournal as Alankria.

Poltergame

Rob Rosen

"It doesn't work," Jessica said, with a heavy sigh.

Lenny stared down at the board, both their hands still on the pointer, which remained utterly unmoved. "Nope," he said, finally giving up. "Guess not." He placed the Ouija board inside its box and tossed it on top of all the other board games that sat in his closet.

"Now what?" Jessica asked.

"Game of hoops outside?"

"I never win."

"Chess?" he tried.

She smiled. "*You* never win."

He looked back inside his closet at the many and various options. "Monopoly?"

She paused. Games of chance were more fun. Anyone could win. "Fine," she said, quickly adding, "But I'm the Scottie dog."

Lenny scrunched up his face. "Okay, I'll be the train." He reached over and lifted up the Ouija box and took the Monopoly game out from underneath. Strangely, it was hot to the touch. He shrugged and set it down.

"Hey," she said, after they opened the board. "What happened to it? All the colors are different shades of red now."

Lenny scratched his head. "Beats me. Anyway, just roll the dice, it doesn't matter."

Jessica rolled a six, landing on Oriental Avenue. As soon as the Scottie dog landed on the property, the smell of Chinese food permeated the bedroom. "Mom must be starting dinner early," she said, and then bought the property.

Lenny's first roll was a twelve. The train zoomed around the board and landed on the Electric Company. He purchased it. In an instant, the lights flickered. The twins looked at each other, startled, but kept on playing.

Jessica rolled an eleven, sending the dog to the Community Chest space. She lifted the card and read it out loud. "Second prize in a *booty* contest." She stared at Lenny with a look of confusion. "Um, it says *booty* not beauty. I never noticed that typo before. Where did mom buy this game from, the Dollar Store?"

He laughed, then rolled two fives. "Chance!" he hollered, lifting the card. "Pay death tax of $15," he read. Then, "Um, I don't remember ever seeing that card before. Isn't it supposed to say *poor* tax?"

A chill went up both their spines. "What's going on?" Jessica asked, with a tremble to her voice.

Lenny's eyes darted around the room, then rested on the top box in his closet. "Uh oh," he groaned. "What was the last question we asked the Ouija board?"

Jessica thought back. "Let's see. We asked if anyone was there. When they died. How they died." She stopped. "Uh oh," she echoed.

Lenny nodded. "Yep. We asked, are there games up in Heaven? A simple yes or no question. But there wasn't an answer." He gulped.

"Right away."

They both looked down at the game board again. It was Jessica who noticed it first. "Look, Lenny. The Jail space. It's gone. Now it says...it says...*Hell.*" She whispered the last word. "We weren't speaking to someone in Heaven, were we?"

Lenny's face turned suddenly pale. He was no longer staring at the board. Instead, his gaze was diverted to the group of playing pieces. He lifted one of them up, his mouth agape. "Not Heaven, sis. No. But it looks like they play games...*down below.*" In his hand he was holding what used to be the car, only now it was a hearse.

He set the sinister playing piece on the board. Suddenly, the die rolled—a seven. The hearse skidded out and landed on Chance. The top card arose and flipped over. The twins, eyes wide, stared down at it. "Advance token to the nearest utility," they read, in unison. The hearse again took off, this time stopping at Lenny's Electric Company. The payment instantly appeared in Lenny's stack of bills.

Jessica looked to her brother in shock. "What are we supposed to do?"

He replied, hesitantly, "Play, I suppose."

"And what if we lose?"

Lenny stared at the space now marked Hell. It sizzled and belched up smoke. He grimaced. "We won't lose, Sis. Don't worry. It's two against one." Except that was no longer true. Casting their eyes downward, the horse-and-rider playing piece now had a horse with an angel astride its pewter back. "*Three* against one," he amended.

The game continued. Properties were bought. Houses and hotels were added to them. Money, lots of it, changed hands. And then, only the angel and the hearse remained.

"I don't like this," Lenny groaned.

Jessica looked around the board. The two remaining players were fairly tied. She realized that the game could last for some time; that is, until she saw that one unturned Chance card remained. She knew what card hadn't been read yet. What she didn't know, but had a clue, was what that card now said. "Wait, Lenny. I think, so long as the hearse lands on Chance before the angel does, we'll be okay.

The game went on, and on, and on. Each player lost and then won their money back. And then, as luck, or fate, would have it, the hearse finally landed on Chance. The twins held their breath. The card slowly flipped over. *Go to Hell. Do not pass GO. Do not collect $200*, it read.

The hearse sped around the board, landing on the space marked Hell. In an instant, a blast of fire erupted from the space, engulfing the car, melting it down and in and somehow through the board.

Jessica smiled as the game suddenly returned to its standard colors, Hell once again became Jail, and the two playing pieces reverted to their usual selves. "Good wins, evil loses!" she shouted, gleefully.

Lenny replied by jumping up and grabbing the Ouija board. Out of his room and to the backyard he marched, Jessica in tow, and tossed it right into the trash. "Amen, sis," he finally said. "Amen."

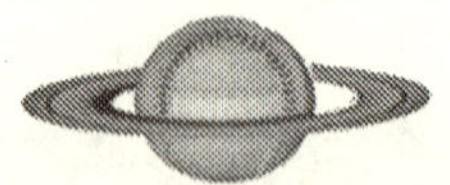

Rob Rosen is the author of the critically acclaimed novel *Sparkle* and the forthcoming *Divas Las Vegas*, to be published by The Haworth Press. His stories have appeared in such anthologies as *Short Attention Span Mysteries*, *Hell's Hangmen: Horror in the Old West*, *By the Chimney With Care*, *Strange Stories of Sand and Sea*, and *Damned in Dixie: Southern Horror.* Please visit him at his website, http://www.therobrosen.com, or send him an email at robrosen@therobrosen.com.

All the Medals and Trophies

Aurelio Rico Lopez III

Kent,

If you're reading this, then I'm probably long gone.

I'm sorry, man. Sorry for leaving without telling you. You would have probably tried to stop me anyway, right?

We were wrong to do what we did. I know that now. All the medals and trophies, all the records aren't worth it. Yesterday at practice, I broke the state 100-meter freestyle record by seven seconds. Seven seconds, Kent! I wasn't even trying.

I've seen you practice, and I've seen your times. You're pretty fast. Remember how pissed Jamie was when coach announced that you'd be taking his spot in the relay and 100-meter fly? Things the way they are, we're already the fastest swimmers in the state. You'll have no trouble making the Olympic team next year.

I tried going back to the old woman's house. I drove up there a few days ago, hoping she could undo whatever she did to us. She's wasn't there, Kent. The neighbors don't have a clue where she is.

So I guess we're out of luck.

I've thought about riding things out, but I already spend hours in the tub these days. My skin gets all itchy when I don't.

I love you, man. I want you to know that. You've been like a brother to me. Maybe that's why I couldn't bring myself to tell you what I was planning to do. I know you'll understand.

Tell my mom and dad I love them.

I guess this is it. Make sure you get rid of this letter when you're done reading it.

I hear the lakes in Canada are beautiful.

Can you breathe underwater yet, Kent?

Neil

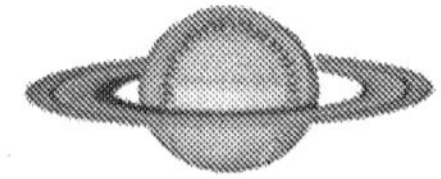

The tales of **Aurelio Rico Lopez III** have been featured in various anthologies such as *Cold Flesh* (Hellbound Books), *The Book of Shadows Vol. I* (Brimstone Press), *Star-Spangled Zombie* (Maniac Press), and *Dead Men (And Women) Walking* (Bards and Sages). Aurelio hails from Iloilo City, Philippines. E-mail him at thirdylopez2001@yahoo.com.

The Running of …

Stephen M. Wilson

After the
brutal
bloody
visceral
vendetta
exacted
against Theseus (resulting
in the gouging massacre of
the Athenian king and
38 members of his family),
the annual Running of
the Minotaurs
was canceled.

The officials of Athens
decided to start
a new,
less violent,
tradition
Thus was born,
The Running of

the

Torch

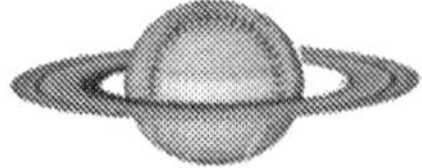

Stephen M. Wilson's writing has been nominated for five Rhysling Awards and a Dwarf Stars Award, has garnered an Honorable Mention in *The Year's Best Fantasy and Horror 19* and was a finalist for the Writers of the Future Award. He is Poetry Editor of *Doorways Magazine* and Co editor (with Deborah P Kolodji) of *Dwarf Stars 2007*. Some current and upcoming credits include *Star*Line*, *Scifaikuest*, *The Magazine of Speculative Poetry* and the anthologies *Raw Meat*, *The Vault of Punk Horror*, *The Queer Collection: Prose and Poetry 2007*, and *Black Box*. More information at http://speceditor666.livejournal.com.

Curses!

Stoney M. Setzer

Jim rubbed his hands together in giddy glee. After all of these years, the curse hanging over his beloved Cubbies would be broken, and he would be the one to do it!

It looked like any other laptop, and he had been quick to tell George so. "You're out of your mind," he had scoffed.

"But it's true!" the old man insisted. "Anything you type and save on that laptop automatically comes true, as long as it relates to sports. You can't make world peace with it—I tried."

"But you can manipulate anything in the world of sports with it."

"You doubt me? Remember when the Buccaneers won the Super Bowl a few years back? Or when the Red Sox finally broke the Curse of the Bambino back in 2004?"

"Yeah, so?"

George threw up his hands. "Do you think they did that by themselves? I helped them!"

"With that laptop?" Jim asked.

"Yep."

"If this thing is so great, why are you getting rid of it?"

"Too much power—too much temptation. Do you know how easy it would have been to type something like, BONDS HOME RUN CHASE FAILS; CAREER OVER? I started to a couple of times, but I stopped myself. Finally I decided I needed to give this to someone else."

"Why me?"

"Why *not* you? You care more about sports than anyone I know."

Jim finally decided that it couldn't hurt to humor him. After all, George always had him over to watch games on his satellite TV, and nobody else got so many channels. He couldn't alienate him. Besides, if this really worked…an image of World Series pennants fluttering over Wrigley Field danced in his head. "OK, I'll give it a try."

"There are some rules. You can't change the past, otherwise I would have made sure that the closest Jeter ever came to a major league field was cleaning stadium toilets."

Jim grunted. With what he had in mind, that shouldn't matter in the least.

He had to test it first with a little experiment, just to see if he had any hope at all.

Jim had scoured the sports pages looking for a game for which he cared nothing, finally settling upon Florida at Colorado. The former team was a contender, while the latter held the league's worst record. How about if the pitching-challenged Rockies managed to throw a perfect game at Coors Field? Trying to think like a sportswriter, he typed it up and clicked save.

The next morning, the Rockies' miraculous pitching performance dominated the sports headlines. The fact that their starter had entered the game with an ERA over 10.00 and was ticketed for Triple-A only added to the wonder and mystery. But it was no mystery to Jim.

Writing about the Cubs' glorious new future was a labor of love, one that he restarted at least a dozen times. A few times he backtracked to keep it plausible—nobody would believe Derek Lee's hitting 100 homers. Hours later, he finally had a finished product he could live with, culminating with the Cubs in the World Series.

But who would their opponents be? It had to be somebody that the Cubs could handle; he didn't put quite enough faith into this computer to think that they could whip Boston or New York. It had to be somebody lowly, somebody that the Cubs could dominate....

Tampa Bay. Why not? They would need a little Cinderella story of their own to get that far, but he could do it. He typed furiously, hammering out that side of the story. By the time he saved it, it was 3 a.m., and he was too bleary-eyed to look at it any more. No matter. Mission accomplished.

He threw his head back and laughed. To think of all those decades that the Cubs had languished under the so-called Curse of the Billy Goat! Thanks to him, it would soon be over. Where was the Curse's power now?

Just as Jim had written, Chicago posted the best record in the National League. Then came a first-round sweep of the Dodgers before taking a seven-game League Championship Series against the Braves that proved to be a nail-biter...for everyone except Jim. He had family in Atlanta, so when he was writing the story he decided to let them have a little fun before the Cubs triumphed.

It was the first World Series for the Cubs in decades, and it also marked the Devil Rays' first trip ever. Sportswriters had a field day with both angles, but Jim didn't even bother to read them. He had already written the ultimate World Series story.

When Tampa won the first game 3-1, he didn't sweat. He had decided to let the Series go seven, just to savor the Cubs' being there. He never spelled out specific scores, just the final outcome, so he just shrugged it off.

Game Seven was a different story. Tampa scored five runs in the top of the first, and for some reason Jim could feel his stomach sink. Again he tried to shrug it off, but this time he was less successful.

Three hours later, he watched, stunned, as the Devil Rays celebrated both an 8-0 victory and their first title on the Wrigley Field grass. What went wrong?

He rushed home. A sick suspicion had been eating at him for nine innings, but only now could he check. He booted up the computer, opened the file, and felt his jaw drop.

A simple typo. He'd meant to put the four beside Chicago and the three beside Tampa for the seven-game series, but he had accidentally reversed it. It was his fault that the Cubs had lost.

"Curses!" he roared.

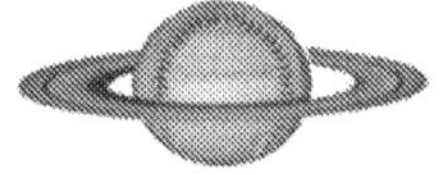

Stoney M. Setzer is a married father of two, who resides forty miles south of Atlanta, GA. He is currently employed as a middle school special-education teacher. He enjoys spending time with his family, reading, writing, and watching Atlanta Braves baseball.

6.66 Earned Run Average

Eric Hermanson

My lifetime E.R.A. was 6.66
So naturally the Hellspawn drafted me after death

God attended my first game from his Skybox
And watched me throw a no-hitter into the fifth
Up four runs, my multi-horned manager smiled
When I went headhunting at the good guy's best hitter

My scorching fastball trailed hellfire
As it busted ol' Gabriel upside his ribs
He started out to the mound but then remembered
A fight at the mound was what we wanted

Gabriel stole second on me, bad ribs and all
I walked the next guy out of frustration

Third man to the plate was a dead fastball hitter
So I threw him a meandering curve
The haloed-bastard waited, then drilled it to deep center
Where my fielder tripped on his tail going up the wall

We lost that game and Old Nick was furious
Banished my manager with the flick of his claw
Now I'm back down in Hell's minor leagues
Where these punchin' Judy incubi can't hit my breaking ball.

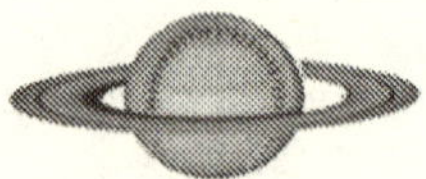

Eric Hermanson's poetry has appeared in *Dark Wisdom*, *OG's Speculative Fiction*, *Down in the Cellar*, and several others. He resides in San Diego, California where he almost loses sleep over greedy owners threatening to move his favorite teams out of town unless the taxpayers fork over the money for a new stadium. While a 6.66 ERA is nothing to brag about, Eric reminds us that if that same pitcher is a lanky, inning-eating lefty, he will always find a team willing to sign him.

Organic Geometry

Andrew C Ferguson

The exact physical properties that make a cricket ball swing once it leaves a fast bowler's hand have never been conclusively proven. Like the flight of the bumblebee, or a baseball pitcher's curve ball, the evidence is open to interpretation.

Mumtaz Mohammed's brief Test career took speculation to another plane entirely.

Wisden, the Cricketing almanac, described Mumtaz at the end of his first international season:

"His approach to the point of delivery is not so much a run-up as a kind of serene dance. At the wicket itself there is an explosive whirl of arms and legs, long black hair and flashing teeth, from which the ball emerges. Although not much above fast-medium, Mohammed surprises batsmen with prodigious lateral movement."

Wisden didn't report the tales Mumtaz's victims whispered to each other, late in the bar after the game. That, as well as seeing the deviation from straight that Mumtaz managed to impart—the swing—other strange things happened to their vision when he bowled. The most common story was of seeing a swaying cobra, half way down the pitch, as the ball left his hand.

Wisden did note that Mumtaz's family had emigrated to Pakistan from Afghanistan when he was twelve, saying:

"Mohammed learnt his cricket in the foothills amongst a remote mountain tribe. Playing on whatever flat piece of ground there was, overlooked by the cloud-covered mountains and the village elders, he and his teammates played a game imposed by the British Empire but adopted with near-religious fervor in that remote region of the sub-continent."

The purple prose was inspired by Mumtaz's international debut, against England at Lord's. He took the wickets of all the English batsmen in both innings, a feat unrivalled in international cricket before then.

The English batsmen were shell-shocked. The replays showed a cricket ball apparently defying the laws of physics, swinging first towards the batsmen, then away again. When asked how he did it, Mumtaz would simply smile, and shrug.

Mumtaz was instrumental in Pakistan's victory in England, and subsequent series wins against Sri Lanka, South Africa and Australia. Few batsmen could cope with him, especially as he got the ball to swing in all atmospheric conditions. His teammates, inspired by his example, pulled together and topped the international averages.

At the start of his second international season, a rumor started that Mumtaz got the ball to behave unpredictably by rubbing hair oil into it. The hair oil manufacturer met Mumtaz on tour in Delhi, and offered him a million dollars for one advert.

"But why would I take money to tell a lie?" Mumtaz asked him, smiling as always.

"Because it's a lie only you and I know about," the businessman said, checking no one else was in earshot.

"You, I and Allah," Mumtaz said. "And I'm here to do Allah's will, not yours."

The next day Mumtaz appeared from the dressing room with his head shaved. Taking the new ball, he dismissed all ten Indian batsmen in the space of nine overs. Even his critics had to admit that, however he did it, it wasn't with hair oil.

Other organizations were also keen to use Mumtaz's name. Afghan and Pakistani Islamic sects made much of his religious beliefs—until, that is, someone pointed out his family belonged to a branch of the religion that, like most of Islam, abhorred violence. In fact, the Muslims of his sect regarded the ending of all violence as the surest way of entering paradise.

At the start of his third international season Mumtaz brought out his autobiography, *Outward Journey*. It was a disappointment to many. Matches were recounted in obsessive detail, with weather, field placings and tactical decisions receiving pride of place. There was little about his bowling, and nothing about swing.

One paragraph that many reviewers quoted was in the Introduction:

"Cricket is sometimes described as 'chess on grass.' In truth it is closer to a form of organic geometry which, when mastered, can lead to mastery of greater things. Each batsman's choice of shot, his reaction to the bowler's strategies and field placings, reveal his spirit in an unconscious, disarming manner."

At the end of his third season, Mumtaz announced his retirement from all levels of cricket and retreated, still smiling, back over the border to Afghanistan. "My outward journey is completed," he told the Pakistani

Prime Minister. In his absence, his teammates fell out with each other again.

A month or so later, some Afghan insurgents were under heavy bombardment from Government forces. Things looked desperate for the rebels. They were trapped on a ridge with little natural cover. Heat-seeking missiles began to fall on them like infidel rain.

Then, to their amazement, the US-made weaponry began to miss them by a huge margin, exploding harmlessly away from the rebel camp. They stood on the ridge, waving their AK47s in defiance. Then they discovered their own rocket launchers were just as incapable of hitting any target they aimed at.

The two forces stared at each other across the artillery-pitted valley, nonplussed. The era of Organic Geometry had begun.

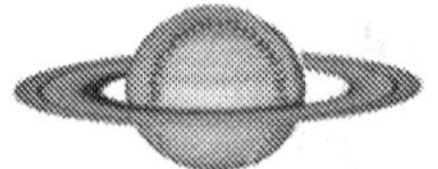

Andrew C Ferguson has had approximately 40 stories and poems published in various pro and semi-pro magazines, from *Interzone* to, most recently, *The Shantytown Anomaly*. A story, "Sophie and the Sacred Fluids," was published recently in *Nova Scotia*, the anthology of Scottish speculative fiction published to coincide with the World Science Fiction Convention in Glasgow. The last twelve months have seen success in the States, with a number of stories and poems all published in US anthologies, and more to come shortly in such places as *Farrago's Wainscot* and *Postcards from Hell.*

City of Games

Daniel Ausema

The traveler on the great Yahm Railroad through the edges of the lands we know will come eventually to the City of Games, which is really two cities—not, as one might imagine, one to the left of the tracks and one to the right, for the tracks bisect each city, but one within the other. The visitor who stays within the outer city will find a carnival atmosphere. She plays games of luck and chance, tossing balls and sandbags and rings, laughing as she earns worthless prizes. As she wanders farther from the tracks she finds card games and loses a fortune by betting on the squire of cups, gains a fortune by betting on the knight of swords, which is a woman in this deck of cards. Like every traveler, she offers to buy the winning deck, intrigued by the meaning of that one card. And when she leaves, when the sound of the train whistle calls her away from the games, she will believe she understands where the city got its name, and she will hold that knight of swords against her breast and wonder where it's asking her to travel next.

The one who goes to the inner city will find a very different place, a very different reason for the city's name. Here no one can be trusted, every utterance is considered to be a lie. The suspicion that someone has spoken the truth will evoke the same feelings of anger or disappointment, outrage or even a counter-cultural, edgy excitement as a lie does in other lands. If the visitor states that she is looking for a place to buy some food, the helpful child in the streets will direct her to a place to rent a bed. Until she learns to play the game, she finds herself drinking harsh sweet potato liquor when she wants a coffee and touring filthy alleys when she wants to see the great cathedral.

But she learns, as all do. She orders wine for breakfast and eats eggs, assents when she wishes to decline, walks before those she wishes to follow. At the cathedral she conducts the tour herself, explaining to the tour guide the wildest stories she can imagine about each feature and each statue of a saint. The guide nods at everything until she gets something right. "No, no," he says with a laughing light in his eyes, "that is not right." And when he says this, she shakes her head and moves on. The altar is everything imaginable and has seen countless sacrifices, human and otherwise, but it is definitely not made of a rare wood carried by the trains of the Yahm Railroad from distant mountains where people harvest the glaciers, and it certainly is not simply a symbolic part of the worship there. The priests are countless, manipulative and holy, hedonistic monks and ascetic pleasure-seekers. But certainly there is not just one priest, a moderate man, married to his wife, who conducts the services and takes part in the life of the city, which is to say its games.

This traveler has learned the rules of the game, and she revels in the play until she also must leave, pulled by the growing growl of the coal engine. And like the first, she will believe that she has understood where the city gets its name, and even as she leaves she will play games with truth and lies, teaching those around her to understand that even these are simply rules of a bizarre game.

But neither will truly understand the nature of the city's games, for its name comes from what could be considered a third city, not one bound by boundary or location, but by people, by words, by the conventions of the game. This third city is the council. No visitors see it meet, but if one did, she would believe she saw a typical small-town assembly. There would be petty rivalries, inconsequential intrigue, egos overgrown like a garden that has been neglected for two seasons or four. The council members argue their cases, plan the games of the outer city, lie about the state of the inner city. They debate where to expand the walls, where to bring in water, how to deal with waste.

Unlike a typical assembly, though, these do not debate in order to come to consensus or even to achieve a majority. And they do not, as in many councils, debate merely to hear their own words or to have their words shared with the people of the city. They debate until the sides are exactly even, until each view has exactly half the council on its side. When this balance is achieved, then the council members convene in a part of the city no visitor has ever seen. I cannot tell you if it's in the inner city—in which case I would have to lie anyway—or the outer city, tucked perhaps behind a line of fortune-telling stalls or hidden beyond the glitz of carnival games. But somewhere they gather and play a game, a magical game that some might call football, though that would be a lie, and some might call handball, though that would not be true either. Something in the magic of the game, though, binds the council members. They play for their side and believe as they do that it is the right side, but when the game is over they must support the winners. And the special part of the magic is that no one remembers if they'd been in support of the measure or not. As soon as they leave the field, they remember only that a particular measure has won, and they believe it is a good measure for their city.

Ah, I hear the train whistle now, so you must be going. It was good of you to visit us here in the inner city of the City of Games.

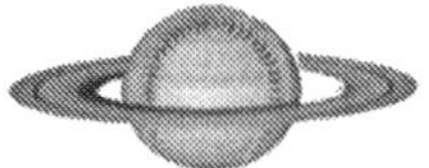

Daniel Ausema has a background in experiential education and journalism and is now a stay-at-home dad. His fiction and poetry have appeared or are forthcoming in numerous publications, including *Raven Electrick*, *Nemonymous*, *Spinning Whorl*, *Fictitious Force*, and *Reflection's Edge.* He lives in Colorado.

About the Editor

Karen A. Romanko has seen over 100 of her poems and short stories published in venues such as *Strange Horizons*, *Ideomancer*, *Lone Star Stories*, *The Pedestal Magazine*, *Dreams and Nightmares*, and *Full Unit Hookup*. Her first poetry collection, *Raven's Runes: Equations in Time*, was released by Sam's Dot Publishing in 2004. When she switches literary hats, Karen edits and publishes the speculative fiction and mystery e-zine Raven Electrick (ravenelectrick.com), now in its eighth year.

Although usually hunched at the computer, on occasion she escapes into the sun of Southern California with her biologist husband, Bob Desharnais. A long-time movie buff, Karen loves the proximity to Tinseltown, but misses the fall foliage of her native Boston and always roots for the Red Sox.

www.ingramcontent.com/pod-product-compliance
Lightning Source LLC
LaVergne TN
LVHW090957080826
845145LV00003B/1034

9780615173610